The
Francie LeVillard
Mysteries

Volume Eleven

The
Francie LeVillard
Mysteries

Volume Eleven

by Tony Seton

Carmel, California
August 2024

These stories are pure fiction – ideas snatched from headlines and whole cloth – and massaged by imagination and driven fingers. While some of the characters are real people – friends who are glad to be in these stories – only some of their participation in the plots or words is based on fact.

The Francie LeVillard Mysteries
Volume Eleven

ISBN-13: 978-1-7325450-7-6

Printed in the United States of America

Table of Contents

The Francie LeVillard Mysteries

Author's Note

This book took a while to write. Not that I was in a hurry, but I find that characters and plots need to percolate. And when they are ready, they pour out through my fingers onto the keys and then up on the screen. It's a wonderful experience. For this reason I have no feeling of writer's block. Perhaps you remember the Paul Masson commercials done by Orson Welles who said they "will sell no wine before its time." The words will pour out when they are ready.

I started writing *The Serra Mob* two years ago. The first scene, at the auto body shop. Then it took a while for the pieces, including a trip to San Jose del Cabo, for it to come together.

Next was *Quaint, But Corrupt,* which was partially instigated by a friend talking about moving to Sea Ranch, up the coast at the northwestern corner of Sonoma County. The essence of the story was about massive, if fictional, corruption in Carmel-by-the-Sea, and some curious twists.

I started writing *The Power Aphrodisiac* because I

thought it was about time to mention Judith Anne, and Hollister provided a new, real-life venue.

Finally, there is *Bang-Zoom*. Originally I was calling it "Baretta" as will make sense when you read the story, but that title didn't cover enough ground as you will see. This story is different in a number of ways, among them that I, who have made a few appearances before, play a significant (understatement) role. Also, I didn't know where it was going...a couple of times, in important directions.

Don't jump ahead. Read the stories – (cough, cough) I mean, case histories – in order.

Thank you.

Tony Seton
Carmel, California
August 2019

Meet Francie LeVillard

Those who are familiar with Sherlock Holmes may remember François Le Villard, the renowned detective who worked in the Deuxième Bureau in Paris, and who collaborated with Holmes on several cases. Francie (she never uses Francine) LeVillard is his great-granddaughter. The space in the last name was dropped by her grandparents because here in America it led to too much confusion.

Francie became a consulting detective after ten years as an award-winning television news reporter on the East Coast where she had grown up. Seeking a change of venue, she took a reporting position at the most-watched station in San Francisco. She was more than disappointed to discover that instead of real journalism, they wanted tabloid "news." The situation became untenable when the news director said he wouldn't renew her contact unless she had a certain cosmetic operation, that the station would happily pay for. The details of that encounter were published in *Francie's First Case* in the second volume.

Needless to say, Francie did not acquiesce, and instead moved to the Monterey Peninsula. It was there – or I should say here – that she made a logical transition in applying her journalistic investigative skills to detective work. It happened serendipitously, and she's been in her new profession for more than a decade now.

Francie is more cerebral than brawny though she is in good physical shape. She trains in aikido three times a week, usually with her best friend and sometime professional partner, Ariane Chevasse, one of the nation's top electronic *spooks*. Francie looks a little younger than 40. Five-seven and 135 healthy pounds, she has a smooth, tan complexion on an oval-ish face framed by dark brown hair that's kept cut in a stylish manner that it will never get in her eyes. She rarely puts on make-up and then very little.

Except on those occasions that call on her to display her natural elegance, Francie dresses for comfort. She wears clothes that allow her to move easily, plus a jacket to hide the pistol she often carries. Either a seven-shot Kel-Tec P32 which fits quietly in a pocket, or if she thinks she might need firepower, she puts a Glock 19 in a holster on the back of her belt. (The Glock is a 9mm semi-automatic with a better operation and greater stopping power than the S&W .357 she used to carry.)

The best description of Francie LeVillard is that she is "bright, attractive, and bad news for bad guys."

The Serra Mob

"I've heard good things about you," Francie LeVillard said, extending her hand to the man with a worldly face.

Gary Bruner was pleased to shake her hand, not just for her words but because he already knew who she was, recognizing her from news coverage as the world's finest consulting detective since Sherlock Holmes. He also knew who had vouched for him. A writer who'd brought his car in for body work and had engaged him in a more than run of the mill conversation .

"I hope that you may share that opinion, Ms. LeVillard."

Francie was only mildly surprised at his reply. She had heard that he was bright and perspicacious, very different from those who had peopled the body shops of yore. She had learned that Bruner had been an insurance investigator for more than a dozen years before "switching sides" to become an estimator at Gene's Import Auto Body. Of course the industry had changed, dramatically, as it had to with the serious attention from both the insurance industry and the state to make sure there wasn't the finagling that had given body shops their tainted reputation.

"I wanted to know, off the record if necessary, what you

might have heard about Serra Spirits." She was watching his face very carefully so she saw a small flicker at his brows on an otherwise perfectly poker face.

He knew she had seen it. The corners of his mouth rose just a bit. With a slight inclination of his head, he directed her to walk with him away from the office door toward an empty portion of the parking lot.

"What is it you thought I might know about that company?"

"I thought you might know from your body shop experience, and perhaps from your investigator days, what kind of operation they ran, the kind of people they hired, the reputation they had...behind their corporate image."

The man was silent for a few steps, keeping his eyes on where he was going. Then he spoke in a soft voice. "Should I ask why you want this information?"

Francie was silent for a moment and then she said, "I could tell you..."

He chuckled, "But you'd have to shoot me?"

She laughed with him and offered, "I thought you might appreciate the deniability."

"There's that. Okay, Serra Spirits. They're a mob business. Have been for forty years. First grandpa who came over from Sicily where the competition was getting a little rough. Then the father, the acorn that fell close to the tree. And now the son, who pretends he's clean."

"But he's not?"

Bruner gave a little snort.

"How so not?"

He shot her a quick glance for the way she phrased the question, not that he didn't understand her. "They used to be Serra Provisions, back before the kid took over. They sold meat and fish all over the Peninsula. The problem was that they got their supplies at a discount because they were 24 to 36 hours old. Sometimes older. That's a long time for such produce to be kept off the flame. The better restaurants told Papa Serra they didn't want old meat and fish. He tried to act tough with them, but a half-dozen of them banded together and made it clear they weren't going to run their businesses into the ground with low-grade food."

"Oh good."

"Yeah, you can't pawn off second-rate food to people who can afford to live around the world, both the locals who comprise 40% of their business, and the tourists who often return year after year. So Papa tried to sell to the lesser establishments at cut-rate prices. That worked for a while, until a few dozen people got sick one night at a big place in Salinas and then at another restaurant three weeks later in Moss Landing. So the company went dark and a month later, came back as wholesalers of wine and spirits. They tried to get the beer distribution but the two companies that were handling the stuff had their own muscle and weren't going to be pushed out."

Francie and Bruner had stopped walking but continued their conversation, facing away from the office toward an empty field.

Francie suggested, "I'm gonna guess that just because they changed their line they didn't suddenly find religion."

"No. They have bought their way into a number of places, good restaurants too, by paying off their buyers, the beverage managers. They also are selling cases of wine that may have been left on a loading dock in the sun. And I heard that sometimes the booze has been watered down a little. Mostly those bottles go to the places with a less discerning clientele."

Francie nodded her head. "So have they tried anything here, with you?"

Bruner shrugged. "People who don't know me will ask for a favor now and then but only once. It might be extra work on a company car because something was their fault. Or to get something done on their personal car and want it charged to the company. Nothing big, but we don't shade the facts. If they ask a second time, I tell them to take their business elsewhere."

"I think everyone wants a favor."

"A favor is okay to ask. It's cheating that's not. I do favors for people. Someone who is gracious and open and asks if some little buffing can be done, sure. Trying to rip someone off doesn't fly with me."

"Tony was right about you, Gary," Francie said as they walked back toward her car.

He turned as they reached the building. He offered her his hand which she took and they shook. He said, "I'm glad we met. Please feel free to call if I can ever be of assistance."

Francie walked around to the driver's side of her car. He followed her and opened her door for her. She got in. "You, too," she said, and he closed her door.

She didn't expect to get a call but it wasn't a week later that her phone rang and the caller ID read "Gary Bruner."

Gary had called to tell her that he had a lead. Actually he didn't say that at all; he didn't even allude to that being the reason for phoning her. But he made it clear that they should get together, and they did. They met at a favorite Thai restaurant in Pacific Grove, Francie arriving a few minutes early as she always did, finding that Gary had gotten a small table in the back from where he could survey the room.

After they had ordered drinks, Gary got right to the point. "You want to know about the Serra mob. The person you need to talk to is Ernesto Rey. He was a supplier of provisions. A wholesaler to wholesalers if you will. He had very good relations with the producers, and they would give him first notice of special deals they had. Maybe it was oversupply, or they saw people wanting something different that they could provide. Ernesto would then notify the people down the line who could act quickly to move the product to their customers; to the restaurants, the markets, and other retailers. But only those who were smart and could act right away because it was all about knowing how to take advantage of trends.

"The Serra people weren't so smart but they were always ready to buy from Ernesto because their customers were smart, and it was from Ernesto through Serra that they got some very good deals."

"But that's when Serra got greedy?"

"Yes, you could almost see it coming, couldn't you?"

Francie nodded.

"At first, as I told you, they tried to muscle their bigger customers, but that wasn't going to work. Then they tried to smear Ernesto. They claimed he had tried to rip them off. But Ernesto wasn't having any of it. This was a guy who had done two tours in Iraq. He'd seen real wars. He went to the restauranteurs personally and told them that he was being pressured to take the fall for the Serra people. It was a good thing that Ernesto had a good reputation and no one bought the Serra's game. Unfortunately, that wasn't the end of it. Someone cut the hydraulics on his car."

"They weren't only crooks, but they were willing to kill someone?"

"Willing yes, but also stupid. The car was on a driveway with a slope, and Ernesto saw the fluid before he got into the car."

"Thank goodness."

"Yeah, but he knew that they wouldn't stop there so he packed a bag and disappeared."

"Did he leave a trail?"

Bruner shook his head. "Not that anyone I know could follow. See, the Serra mob not only wanted to make him the fall guy, Ernesto was a threat because he knew too much about them. If he had wanted to, he could have gone to the police and caused a whole lot of trouble for them. And they knew it."

"Sounds like he was smart to leave."

Bruner nodded his agreement.

"How long ago was this that he left?"

"Three, maybe four years ago."

"And Gary, you have no idea where Ernesto might be found?"

"No. I don't think he wanted to be found, by the wrong people."

"Where was he from?"

Bruner shook his head.

"Was he an American?"

"I don't know if he was born here, but he spoke without any accent."

"But he could speak Spanish?"

"Oh yeah. And some Italian." He chuckled. "He made friends with a lot of the fishermen."

"And did you know him personally?"

"I did. It wasn't like we were close, but we knew each other, respected each other. He was a good guy. I hope he still is. Good I know, he always would be. I mean alive."

*　　*　　*　　*　　*

Having worked successfully on a number of cases in the Monterey area, Francie had developed quality professional relationships with both the sheriff and the FBI's regional managing agent for the area. As the collaborations increased, and she had demonstrated both her considerable investigative skills and remarkable intuitive abilities, they had extended to her access to various online databases that state and national law enforcement used, including financial and judicial records, fingerprint and passport files.

When Francie had returned home from her meeting with Gary Bruner, she'd started looking for Ernesto Rey. This had gone beyond wanting to make a case against Serra Spirits for what they had done to my car – hitting it and getting the driver and a friend to lie about it – but it could be an opportunity to rid the neighborhood of a bad actor.

She started from nowhere, as investigators described this type of search, with his name, which she knew was not uncommon, and Monterey. She thought he might have filed a police report on the vandalism to his car but there was nothing. He was probably just focused on getting out of town. She did get a hit on a bank account at Monterey County Bank; the account had been closed out around the time that he was supposed to have fled.

What was valuable here was that the information on the bank account included his address, date of birth, and Social Security number, and it was with these data that Francie discovered that Ernesto Rey had a passport. And that he had used it to cross the border to Mexico, specifically San Jose del Cabo. She also found that his fingerprints, matching those from his military service, had surfaced on a job application with a firm in Las Vegas that did the hiring for the Grand Mayan resort. With that, Francie was able to learn that Ernesto Rey had kept his name, and was working as the manager of one of the resort's restaurants, Casa Calavera.

*   *   *   *   *

"You really need to do something about your airport," Francie LeVillard said to the manager of the Grand Mayan resort in San Jose del Cabo. "I know it's not the city's, it belongs to the Baja California Sur state, but it's your name on it."

"What about our airport?" Jose Montrino asked surprised. "It is rated one of the top facilities in all of Latin America."

"Perhaps it is because you are a Mexican citizen, but for those of us coming from outside your country, we have to run a gauntlet of hucksters trying to get us to buy timeshares."

Montrino frowned. "I have not seen it but I have heard about it. You are not the first person to speak to me about it."

"When I cleared customs, I wanted to go back to the car rental area, but they wouldn't let me. It wasn't a security issue. They sent me through a very large room with long counters and men looking at the tourists like we were their prey. When I asked someone about where I should go to pick up my rental car, not one but two different people walking around in the area told me to see one of the people behind the counters. But they weren't going to tell me how to get to the car rental location. They just wanted to pitch me on a timeshare."

"Señorita, we have in the rooms an *aviso* about these hucksters as you call them. They are everywhere. They offer a deal that is too good to be true, and they coerce people into signing up. It happens in many places. We have been asking the state to clean them out of the airport as it gives our visitors a bad impression of del Cabo. They say they are working on it, but it will take maybe five years."

Francie gave the man a half-smile. "We have corruption like that in our country, too, but it's more subtle."

"I am very sorry for your experience."

Francie was silent for a long moment as she looked into the man's eyes, assessing both his sincerity and his authority. "I know you are just the manager of this resort, but perhaps you will pass on to the owners that this does not help you to attract more guests. You don't want people returning to their homes and telling their friends about their first experience of Cabo."

"I will communicate that with the owners as you suggest," he said with a sense of relief in the voice. Then he gave her a deep smile. "Now please tell me, how I can make your stay a better one. No," he held up his hand. "Make this the best holiday you have ever had."

Francie sighed. "Thank you, but I'm here only for a few days." She gazed through the huge windows that looked out onto the resort and its inviting beach and the Sea of Cortez beyond. "I wish it would be longer." She turned back to the manager. "Another time it will be for pleasure, Señor Montrino."

She noted the flicker of a question in his eyes, and to

assuage his concern told him, "I'm a writer. I decided to put one of my characters in this location."

Not assuaged, but delighted at the obvious chance to promote his facility, Montrino held up a finger, "Momento," he said. And he looked down at the computer terminal on the counter in front of him. He played with the keyboard for a few seconds, and then looked back at Francie. With a fake frown he said, "I'm afraid your room is not ready. However," he added quickly, "I have a suite that I think you will find to your liking."

"Oh, thank you," Francie enthused, pretending to be surprised. His fingers worked over the keys and soon the printer next to the monitor produced a registration form. He handed it to Francie. The new accommodations were clearly a high-priced upgrade, but the rate was half of what she would have been charged on her original reservation.

"You are too kind, Señor Montrino, but I can't accept this."

"But you must, Señora," his smiled insisted.

"Señorita," Francie corrected, returning the smile.

"Señorita. A woman so beautiful, in our country she would have to be married."

"How nice of you to say."

"But please, accept our hospitality. It is in appreciation for your concern about our image in del Cabo. It is very important what you have told me, and I will forward it to our owners. They have the influence with our government."

"Well, if you put it that way, then I can accept. Thank you."

"Thank you," he insisted. Then he took a ribbon with an electronic key, programmed in a device connected to the computer, and handed it to her along with a business card he took from his wallet. "Please, Señorita, be sure to contact me personally if there is any need you might have. Call any time. I am at your service."

A few minutes later, Francie had been conducted to her suite on the top floor with a stunning view of the sand and the Sea of Cortez. It was late afternoon, and the early fall sun was into its descent to the horizon. Francie unpacked her things and put on shorts, a light top, and sandals and headed for the beach. The sand was warm, not hot, so she shed the sandals and walked the beach at the water's edge, enjoying the soft lap of the waves that occasionally would come in up to her knees.

Having been a broadcast journalist for ten years before she became a consulting detective a decade earlier, she not only knew how to spin a yarn – and on the spot – but it came easily to her. Yes, she could write a travel piece on her trip to this beautiful spot, and take a well-deserved shot at the hucksters, trying to corral unsophisticated tourists into signing up for shady deals, but that was not the reason for her trip.

*   *   *   *   *

The next day, Francie dropped into the restaurant shortly after it opened at eleven for lunch, presuming that being the manager was principally a day job. She ordered a glass of sangria and started in on the best chips and guacamole she had ever tasted. When the waitress came to the table for her lunch order, Francie told her, all with a big smile, how much she enjoyed the chips and guacamole, and noting that she was a travel writer, asked if she might speak to the manager. The waitress, smiling back, said she would see if he was available.

It was less than two minutes later that Ernesto Rey approached her table. Francie knew it was he, even though he had changed his look from the way Gary Bruner had described him. The Army cut and clean face had been covered with a full but sculpted head of black hair, and a trim mustache and van dyke bread. The man certainly enjoyed Francie's appearance, but he wasn't intrusive about it. He stood in front of her table and confirmed she had asked for him.

"Yes, and I hope you would have a few minutes for me," she told him, gesturing for him to take the seat opposite.

He looked around, apparently confirming that there were no other patrons in the restaurant, and took the seat. He peered at her as if he might recognize her.

"The resort manager here knows me to be a travel writer. But you may have seen my photograph in the paper, when you lived on the Monterey Peninsula."

His look at her hardened.

Taking a business card out of her pocket and pushing it slowly across the table, she told him, "My name is Francie LeVillard. I'm a consulting detective. You have no need to be alarmed. You know Gary Bruner. I was having a drink with him just last week. If you called him right now, he would tell you that you can trust me. I'm not here to reveal your presence or to in anyway cause you danger."

She was impressed to see that he took in her words the way she meant them, and that Bruner had been an important, calming reference.

"I might ask how you found me," he began after a moment of taking her in, "but my first question would be why you were looking for me."

"Good for you. I'll answer both questions, but the why is because a friend of mine was in a traffic accident with a Serra truck. No one was hurt, but that's how I met Gary Bruner. We had an interesting conversation, and I was prompted to see what might be done to take the Serra mob down. I don't like crooks. I don't like people trying to kill people for telling the truth. Especially cutting a hydraulic brake line which could have resulted in not only your death but the death of others who had no connection to you or them. I'm not asking – I'm not suggesting – that you go back to Monterey. But I think you have information that could help me put an end to their criminal racket."

Francie sat back in her chair. "I'd like to make it safe for you to return, if you wanted, although," she added with a sincere smile and gesturing around the restaurant, "I could see why you might want to stay here."

Rey took a long time looking at the consulting detective before he spoke. "How did you find me?"

"Because of my work, and what I've accomplished on behalf of law enforcement, both state and federal, I've been granted special access to personal files that are not available to the general public. The fact that you didn't change your name helped. But it was Gary's description of who you are – your good character – that made me want to find you."

He took a deep breath and let it out slowly. "There is no privacy anymore."

"Very little," Francie agreed.

Again he was silent for almost two minutes. But Francie wasn't about to hurry him.

"Am I safe here?"

"I would think so. You've changed your appearance. Also, you left their stage. Why should they see you as a threat?"

He cocked his head slightly to one side, as if to get a different perspective on her. "What if someone here recognized you? I did, at least I knew I'd seen your picture. And what if they saw you with me? That could be a problem."

"Yes, it could. Though I don't know the odds of that happening. There could also be people who knew you in your past life coming to this resort."

"I'm careful to stay out of view as much as I can." He was trying to make a case for his security, but it wasn't getting much traction in the moment.

"Mr. Rey, whether you want to go back to Monterey some time, or you want to stay here for the rest of your life...or find another place to hide, the fact is that you will only be safe when the Serra mob is in prison. I believe you have information that I can use to make that happen, and without you going north, or them finding out that you are the source of the information."

"Why do you think I have that kind of information?"

"Because you're that kind of man. You're honest. You value the truth. You believe in justice."

"How do you know that?"

Francie laughed. "Because I believe what Gary told me. And because in the few minutes we've been sitting across from each other, I've seen it in your face."

"I suppose I must defer."

"Good," Francie declared. "Now what can you tell me about the Serra people that can help me put them in prison?"

"Would you like to order some lunch, Señorita? We have very good food here at Casa Calavera. By the way, do you know what is the theme of our restaurant?"

"I did look it up. I believe it celebrates the Day of the Dead, doesn't it?"

"That's right. In this culture, it is called "Día de Muertos," and it is when family and friends pray for those who have died and wish them well on their spiritual journey."

"I must say, seeing all of the skeletal heads, all smiling, was a curious first look, especially for a restaurant at a resort, but knowing the explanation behind it is very soothing."

"That's right. It's very important for people here in

Mexico. Remembrance of those who have departed has deep meaning."

Francie raised her glass. "To the departed," she said, "And to those who remember them on their continuing journey."

Rey steepled his fingertips in front of him and bowed over the gesture. "Thank you, Señorita," he said.

*   *   *   *   *

The meal that was served to Francie was one of the finest she'd ever enjoyed. Rey had the kitchen prepare bites of a dozen different items on the menu, from salmon and octopus to pork and chicken, all prepared according to local recipes. He also switched her over to white sangria made with freshly-squeezed oranges. As he guided her through the delicious smorgasbord, he also gave her information about the Serra mob.

At the end of the amazing array of flavors and textures, Rey offered Francie dessert, and while she insisted she had eaten more than enough, he insisted that she try what he called *Smoked Tres Leches Cake* which, he explained, was house-made sponge cake made with condensed milk, toasted almonds, and Mexican vanilla. She agreed to a taste and asked if she might bring the rest back to her room.

"Of course, Francie." He'd been asked to call her by her name early in the meal. "And let me tell you what a true delight it has been to meet you. And to have you enjoy this special meal at my table."

"Ernesto, the pleasure has been all mine."

"No, Francie, I feel a great burden has been lifted from my shoulders. I love Mexico, and my position here, but I would like to be able to visit my friends on the Monterey Peninsula. You will make that possible."

Francie nodded. "You have certainly given me a lot of information, Ernesto. I think the U.S. attorney will see this as a RICO – a racketeering – case. That's a more serious case than just a state prosecution."

He looked down at his hands together on the table in front of him. When he looked up at Francie, his eyes were twinkling. "I have a big dessert for you."

"Oh no, really, I am already stuffed."

He leaned forward and said quietly, "Not that kind." He saw her perplexed expression, and then told her, "I have a recording."

Francie sat up and slowly leaned across the table and waited.

"There was a meeting of the five top members of the Serra company. It was a dinner at the house of the *jefe*. They talked for almost an hour and a half about their operations and who was going to run which one and how."

"Holy moly," Francie said, but then winced. "But they didn't know you were taping them, of course. It wouldn't be allowed to be presented as evidence."

"I didn't do the taping. It was done by *el jefe*. It was his life insurance. He told everyone at the table about the recording. He said if anything happened to him other than dying naturally, it would go to the police."

"Oh my goodness. And no one objected?"

"They couldn't. They might not make it to their home that night."

"How did you get the recording?"

"I didn't actually receive it, not directly. I learned that it was put online and I copied it."

"Where is it now?"

He reached inside his shirt and took out a small leather billfold. He opened it and withdrew a small piece of paper that had been laminated. He held it up for Francie to see. On it was written a short series of letters and numbers that end in "mp3."

He tore off a piece of the menu and copied the URL to it. He folded it and handed it to Francie. "You will need the password which is very simple. Capital E-9-3-9-4-2-capital R. My initials with my post office box zip code in between." He sighed deeply, having been relieved of a long-held burden. "This will put them all in prison, the five at the dinner, and there are names of their lieutenants. Enough so they will turn on each other as fast as they can to get a deal."

"But Ernesto, why didn't you give this to the authorities yourself?"

"Because until now, no one had any idea that I knew about it. If I handed it over, they would find out and my life wouldn't be worth a peso."

"But if I turn it over?"

"You have no connection to the Serra mob. It wouldn't

matter. Me, they know me. They would want to have revenge. You got the recording. They would only care who gave it to you. And you would give it to the authorities saying it arrived anonymously. You can do that, yes?"

Francie nodded her head. "Yes." What she didn't say was it certainly wouldn't be the first time she'd been handed important evidence that she passed along to the U. S. attorney. "Good. All right, Ernesto. I'll take care of this. Thank you."

"Thank you, Francie."

*   *   *   *   *

"Welcome back, Francie. Good trip?" Sheriff Telford "Bogie" Spivac was calling the morning after she had gotten home.

Francie laughed. "Yes. A lovely spot. I thought about stretching it into a vacation, except it was work. But that's probably not why you called, is it?"

"I wish it were. We got word that Ernesto Rey got mugged last night."

"Oh jeez. Is he all right?"

"He will be. A couple of broken ribs and some deep bruises but nothing fatal. Oh, and they didn't take his money."

"Any idea who did it?"

"I kinda figured you might know. All I know is that you met with him two days ago."

"That's right. So he must have been able to tell the police that much."

"Yeah, he told local authorities and they contacted my office. They say it was a sending-a-message mugging."

"But how did Serra's people know I was down there and talking to Ernesto? That's really creepy."

The sheriff was silent, as if he could hear the (consulting) detective thinking.

"It must have been a connection up here. Only a few people knew I was looking into the Serra mob, but I certainly didn't tell anyone I was going to del Cabo, or why I was going."

"Maybe someone saw you down there, saw you talking with him?"

"I suppose that's possible, but what are the chances. I mean, Bogie, I'm not one of the most recognizable of people, especially out of this area. Seems highly unlikely."

"And you haven't seen anyone following you up here? You've got a very good sense if someone is interested in you."

"No, not even a feeling."

"Maybe someone saw you at the airport?"

"Maybe, but all they would know, based on the flight I boarded, was that I was going to Phoenix."

"I wonder if it wouldn't be worth a chat with the airline clerk who checked you in. She issued you the boarding pass to Cabo, right?"

"Yes, she did, and come to think of it, I had a sense that she knew who I was, or at least recognized my name."

"It might be worth a shot. Get her into a room and ask her directly who she gave your information to. That would be hard for her to lie about and not be obvious."

"It's worth a try. I went out on an American flight on Tuesday that left at 9:50 for Phoenix." There was a pause. "I'm trying to remember her name. I think it was Lolita or Rosita. She was young, pretty, early twenties, long dark hair, bright red lipstick."

"That should be enough to find her. I'll send Ursula DeVine. She's sharp."

"Yes, she's good. Thanks for this, Bogie."

"Of course. I would love to bust the Serra mob."

"Yes, so would I." Then in a very different voice, Francie said, "Bogie, we should get together and talk about that."

The sheriff heard her. "I'll be over on the Peninsula for a dinner at Spanish Bay at six-thirty," he suggested, adding, "If that's convenient."

*   *   *   *   *

"We got lucky," the sheriff said, greeting Francie as she joined him at a table in a distant corner of the Sticks bar.

"Ursula?"

He nodded. "She has great bearing, and this girl just crumbled. She brought her into the manager's office, and had her sit down while she stood over her. She said, 'We're investigating an attempted murder, and we have evidence you had a part in it.'"

Francie whistled.

"Yeah," Bogie chuckled. "She turned white and almost slid out of the chair. Ursula told her that she could be charged as an accessory and be facing seven years in prison. The girl started crying and hyperventilating at the same time."

Francie winced. "Ouch."

"Then Ursula changed her tone and told the girl that she could avoid prison if she told her the truth. It took a while for the girl to pull herself together. She said she didn't know. She said a friend of hers came up to her after you had gone through security and asked where you were ticketed to. He said you were a friend of his boss who wanted to send you flowers."

Francie rolled her eyes. "Boggles the mind, doesn't it? Who was the guy?"

"That's the sticky part. He's a first-year lawyer working for the DA. He happened to be meeting someone coming in on another flight when he saw you. You're a more familiar face in those circles. We got him to the DA's office and questioned him. He played dumb, denied talking to the ticket agent."

"And then you checked his phone."

The sheriff looked at her and shook his head. "I don't know how you do that, France, but yes. There were two calls, even before your plane was off the ground, to Serra's warehouse. When we told him he was going to be charged with conspiracy and attempted murder he nearly soiled himself. Apparently his cousin is a dispatcher there, and your name had come up in an earlier conversation. When we pressed him, he admitted he knew from talk in the office that you had been making queries about Serra's operations."

"I guess they made a call to a Cabo affiliate, so to speak, to follow me from the airport, and then to deal with poor Ernesto."

"And this is a small community. The family networks, good and bad, reach everywhere. We certainly know that in law enforcement."

"Well I have a surprise for you, my friend," Francie said, leaning toward him and lowering her voice. "It's the reason why Ernesto was given the warning. The good news is that it came too late." Then she explained what she had learned from Ernesto Rey and about the audio file.

"Holy smokes, that's dynamite."

"It is indeed. I listened to it when I got home, and though I don't speak Spanish, from what Ernesto told me, and what I heard on the recording, this could be the key to blowing up the Serra mob."

"This sounds like a federal case instead of local."

"That was my take. I called Mike but he was up in The City. Coming back tomorrow morning. I made a copy of the audio and parked it in a safe-house site with a different URL and password. I also ran it through a mixer at a slightly different speed and different tracking aspects so it can't be traced to what Ernesto had." She handed the sheriff an otherwise blank card that had the new URL and password. "I wasn't going to leave a phone message, even on Mike's line. But I did tell him he would want to see you first thing."

"I can give it to him tomorrow," he said. He and Mike Olsen, the FBI's managing agent, both had their offices in Salinas.

"Good. It would be neat if this could be all cleared up, enough so Ernesto could come back here safely, at least for a visit, though I know he likes it down there."

*   *   *   *   *

Having heard the audio file, the FBI worked quickly, rounding up both the principals and the secondary mobsters who might have taken control, or fought each other trying to. So it was only two days after he was back in his office that Mike Olsen called Francie to update her on what they had done, and what they had learned in the process.

"The Serra mob wanted Ernesto Rey to be killed. They didn't need to send Rey a message, since he'd already been seen talking to you. They were going to send a message to you that your life was in danger if you pursued the matter."

"So what happened? Why did they only beat him?"

"Well, as luck would have it, one of the muggers had a sister who worked for Ernesto at the restaurant. She had a great job and if Ernesto had been killed, she might have had to work for another manager who demanded, uh, favors from the waitresses."

"Oh my goodness. We have to appreciate the threat of sexual abuse of workers, then? If the threat wasn't there, then Ernesto Rey would have been killed."

"Strange world, isn't it?"

*   *   *   *   *

Later that week, Francie dropped by Gene's Import Auto Body to tell Gary Bruner about what had occurred as a result of their meeting. He got her a cup of coffee and they walked outside to the end of the lot.

"You're a great excuse to get outside, you know?"

"Glad to be of service."

"So what's the story?"

And Francie told him, and in great detail, adding that she had heard from Ernesto Rey who had healed quickly and only missed three days of work. He was delighted and relieved to learn of the incarceration of the people who had been running the Serra mob.

"And so was I, Francie. Those people were on the street far too many years. Mostly because they scared everyone who knew about them so the cops couldn't get a foot in their door. But that's done now. Great."

"I thought you would be pleased, Gary. It's great for the community."

"Not like it will end all the crime in the county, but it will warn off those who think that a tight-knit crime family can get their way anymore. Knock on wood," he added, tapping his knuckles on the side of his head.

"Loyalty doesn't seem to mean what it used to, does it?"

He shook his head. "But maybe that means we have to hold people accountable more, and be more responsible ourselves."

"At least with those people who would share our values,

Gary."

"Yes, ma'am."

"Oh, and I wanted to thank you for talking to the insurance investigator. Tony told me his agent had gotten a reversal from the company on the decision of who was at fault."

"Yeah, you're welcome. Glad to do it. And it wasn't a favor. It was the truth. The evidence was clear that the truck drove into Tony's car. It wasn't his fault at all. The witnesses were either wrong or lying."

"So they will be giving him his deductible back, and going after the Serra driver." She patted Gary on the back. "I like it when the good guys win."

<u>Quaint, But Corrupt</u>

The Sonoma County sheriff's deputy said the body had been found in a shoreline pool, maybe ten feet from the base of the 20-foot bluff. Yes, there were bruises to the head and body, and that would be expected from a fall from that height onto the rocks below. There were no signs of foul play, he insisted, and no indications of a struggle atop the bluff. So the conclusion of the investigation was death by misadventure: Wayne Douglass had fallen to his death. He was 75 years old after all. Perhaps he experienced a moment of dizziness.

But Francie LeVillard, the finest consulting detective since Sherlock Holmes, wasn't buying it. She had known the man for nearly a decade, most of the time when he had been the city administrator of Carmel-by-the-Sea. She had dealt with Douglass not only in his professional capacity, but had known him as a friend; they had been good friends. They would get together at The Cottage for breakfast every other week and talk politics, local and national, and they would talk about people, particularly and generically.

Francie, having been an award-winning broadcast journalist in Our Nation's Capital and New York City for a decade, never lost her hunger for a discussion of current events, and Wayne Douglass was one of the few people she knew – even within the news industry – who kept up on national and international affairs the way she did. He eschewed the term "news junkie" because he wasn't addicted to the news; as Francie noted one morning, he was on top of it. Or the way she described her own interest, she was fascinated to watch history being written.

Douglass had left the Monterey Peninsula only six months before his untimely death, choosing to live in a mostly tourist-free bucolic spot 200 miles up the California coast... The Sea Ranch. He had talked for some time about the privacy and the quiet – the serenity – of a place where he could walk for miles by the Pacific Ocean, and a good distance away from civilization. It was after his retirement, and then a divorce after a long separation, that he finally made the move. He chose a house in the woods on the east side of the Pacific Coast Highway. It was a name from the past, since the "highway" up there is a two-lane road lightly-traveled except over major vacation weekends.

Francie had gone up to visit her friend only a month before his death. She had marveled at the beauty and the light of his three-bedroom house, with its spectacular views of the Pacific, and they had enjoyed several long walks along the bluff – and by the very spot above where his body had been found by other regular walkers.

With her reputation, and the added facilitation of a call from the Monterey County sheriff, her close friend, Telford "Bogie" Spivac, the Sonoma sheriff had agreed to let Francie examine Douglass' home, now three days after his death. This being early October, the weather was clear, and she chose to fly up. The Sea Ranch has a private airstrip, and the Sonoma County sheriff arranged with them for her to use it. They also provided her with a company car to get to Douglass' house and around as otherwise needed.

The deputies had used a key in Douglass' pocket to get into the house. He had shown Francie where he hid a copy of it should she come up at a time when he was not there. It was on a hook on the back of a bird feeder hanging from a pine tree off the back porch. She used it to unlock the back door and enter the house. With her skepticism about the cause of her friend's death, Francie was not greatly surprised to find that someone had searched the house, and it must have happened after the deputies made their entry and done a cursory search since they had reported everything intact.

Whoever had come in afterward had not bothered to cover their traces. Drawers were pulled out, cupboards and closets emptied onto the floor. Francie called the Sonoma sheriff's office and reported what she found. They said they would have someone over in a half-hour, and asked her to stay until they arrived. Meanwhile, Francie compared what she saw in front of her to the mental pictures she had from a month before. It was very obviously not an opportunistic burglar, since fine pieces of art, some expensive jewelry, and high-end entertainment equipment had not been taken.

But there was a glaring omission. Douglass' laptop was missing from his desk. Also gone were two neat piles of manila file folders that had been on the desk. While there was a scattering of pads, pens, and other accoutrements on the floor around his office space, there were no file folders.

Why, Francie asked herself, hadn't whoever made the illegal entry not done so right after killing Douglass? Why had they come back another time? According to the coroner, the body had gone into the water around dusk, which meant that it was unlikely to be spotted until the next morning, which was, in fact, when the 911 call was made. The only possible explanation she could come up with was they thought it would be better to go in after the deputies had checked out his house; that it might give them more time before their foraging would be discovered. She didn't find the speculation wholly satisfactory. All the deputies could offer in explanation were shrugs.

An hour later, after another walk-through of the house, Francie drove to The Sea Ranch offices to turn in the car and to express her appreciation for how well they took care of matters for her friend. Then she accepted a ride to the airstrip. The flight home was an easy one which gave her time to ponder what she had learned, and wonder what she might do about it.

*   *   *   *   *

An answer came late the next morning when she received a call from Hugo Gerstl, her attorney and another important friend in her professional network. His office was to where all FedEx and UPS packages were redirected when she wasn't home to sign for them. She never wanted anything left at her house when she wasn't there. Packages left sitting before her front door were an invitation to the wrong people.

"FedEx dropped something off for you late yesterday. You weren't home. The return address is 'Wayne Douglass'."

"Oh my goodness."

"I didn't know him personally but I know he was a friend of yours and a very good man. Well, he would have to be, wouldn't he?"

"Yes. Thanks, Hugo. I'll be by shortly."

"Should we meet for lunch instead? Is this something your attorney should be present when you open it?"

"Lunch with you is always a good idea, my dear friend. As regards your second question, I'd like to say I don't have any idea what's in it, but it arriving at the time it did, I suspect it might be connected to what happened to him."

"Sur at 11:30?"

"Perfect."

As the restaurant was just opening for lunch, Billy Quon seated them at Francie's favorite corner table. Hugo handed her the FedEx document box.

She examined every aspect of the outside of the box carefully. She noted that the label had been printed. She presumed that Douglass had used a Selectric-type typewriter at The Sea Ranch Lodge office since who owns a typewriter anymore? Especially the kind that can make clear carbon copies on label forms. She also noted that it had been sent the day of his death.

Hugo looked at her with concern. "I'm sure it's safe to open, Francie. I checked. The box hasn't been tampered with."

She might have told him that she was getting a sense of the box, but she knew he was just reassuring her. She was getting a feeling of Douglass, when he was sending it off four days ago, hours before he was murdered. By the weight, she had a good idea what was in the box.

"You know what it is?" Hugo asked.

"I think it's the book he was working on," she said as she finished her examination of the box.

"Not very heavy."

"No, he wouldn't have sent his computer. He wasn't finished with the book." She raised her eyebrows to correct her comment. "He is now, but his book may yet come out. He probably sent a flash drive or portable hard drive."

"I'm sorry," he offered in a condolent voice.

"Yes. What a waste."

"So he must have known he was in trouble."

"He was stirring up a hornet's nest. Something to do with big money down here. I think someone was enriching some of our government officials."

Hugo frowned. "That happens to a lot more than people realize. They think they pay their taxes that go to pay bills, but all too often, sticky fingers pull out a pile for themselves."

"I think this time it's paying the pols to grease the wheels for building permits and inspections." Francie sat back and looked at the box. "I think I'll open it when I get home, Hugo."

"What? I shouldn't know?"

"Hugo, he wouldn't tell me what was going on. That was to protect me." She looked at him meaningfully. It took but a moment and he got it.

"You mean they would have tortured him to find out if he had told anyone else."

Francie shrugged. "Some people are like that."

"I know, look at the Trumpster. Not just supporting wars around the world, but undermining the health of innocent civilians. His people were threatening other countries for encouraging mothers to breast-feed their babies. So his friends running big pharma could make even bigger profits selling them formula. Which, one, they can't afford, and two, isn't nearly as healthy for their babies." Despairingly he added, "What is wrong with our country?"

"Greed is good? I dunno, Hugo," she said with a sigh. "This isn't the world we were brought up to believe in."

"I should have given the box to you after we ate. I was looking forward to a good lunch. I like the food here. Especially what I'm not supposed to eat."

Francie showed him an understanding smile. "Okay, instead of a salad, I think I'll go for comfort food. And a beer. We can toast Wayne."

*   *   *   *   *

Aware that someone might know that Douglass had sent her something they didn't want her to see, Francie took her time driving the six miles south to her home at Yankee Point. She knew how to spot a tail, and with the particularly light mid-week traffic, she was clear that there was no one following her. Still, when she got home, she drove into the garage and closed the door behind her the moment she was inside.

Once in the house, she confirmed through her state-of-the-art security system that no one had come into the house. It also reported that the outdoor cameras had seen nothing out of the ordinary, and her newly-installed back-up generator was fully fueled and on instant turn-over standby. The generator had been added in an underground cinder block structure under her deck when someone trying to warn her off an investigation – or to kill her – had cut her phone and power lines. She also had a satellite dish installed, out of sight, to assure that she could communicate with the outside world, should someone try to isolate her.

She had locked the door to the garage behind her when she walked in, and after resetting the security system to "Perceive" – she smiled at the marketing term – Francie headed across the living area to her office in the south wing of the house and put the box from Douglass on her desk. Then she walked back to the kitchen area and turned on the heat under the kettle. She picked out a bag of a favorite tea and dropped it in a mug. Then she returned to her desk.

With another sigh, she took an Exacto knife from the pencil holder on the back of her desk and carefully slit the tape holding the box closed. Douglass had also taped all of the edges as well, and with his own tape, not what FedEx supplies. The seams were untouched. Inside, she discovered a two-terabyte portable hard drive wrapped several times in bubble wrap, a 256 GB USB 3.0 flash drive also carefully wrapped, and an envelope. She put the drives on her desk in their packaging, and slit the envelope. Before taking out the letter inside, she tilted her head back against the top of her chair and stared unseeing at the ceiling.

It wasn't long before she heard the whistling of the kettle. It pulled her out of her reverie and then to the kitchen. She filled the waiting mug, took a spoon from the dish strainer, and with the envelope from Douglass walked into the living room. She eased into her favorite oversized leather chair, depositing her mug and the spoon on the table beside her. Then she removed the letter from the envelope. It was printed. Douglass always joked that with his handwriting, he should have been a doctor; but he was no good at the sight of blood, especially his own. That memory had surfaced at a particularly inopportune moment and generated an unladylike verbal attack on those responsible for his death.

She shook her head to free herself from the anger, and focused on what he had written:

My dear Francie,

It was with considerable trepidation that I decided to make you the recipient of this letter.

I knew it would likely put you in jeopardy, but I've never known anyone – man or woman – with the mind and skills that you have; that you have demonstrated over the years. I have often remarked about your competence and strength. You will need it, dealing with these people. I would have told you in person but there wasn't time. And now I've moved on to my next life.

The files on the hard drive and the flash drive are the same. They are what I've been using to write my book. If the worst happens, I'm relying on you to get the information out.

The evidence, including documents that show two sets of books, reveals how a group of foreign investors got contractors to build shoddy new houses and renovations in Carmel that wouldn't show their defects for a few years. They bought sub-standard sheetrock from a firm in China that showed up in expensive new building on the Florida Gulf coast and needed to be replaced. It was the same company that sold FEMA the formaldehyde trailers after Hurricane Katrina hit New Orleans.

These contractors also used second-rate cement in the foundation that will start crumbling in another two years. They got a great price on miles of PVC pipe that were left sitting on a dock in the Mexican sun getting brittle. So all the interior pipes they have installed in some thirty houses in Carmel will have to be replaced. Also, the wiring was bought from a firm in India whose products have been banned from sale in the U.S. because they don't pass our fire standards. You'll find the details of all this on the drives.

This is just part of the story. The local contractors were really foolish. They were supposed to be paid off at the time of the properties being finished, but the controlling top contractors – the money people – claimed there was a problem with their bank and there would be a delay. Of course, they had no intention of paying the contractors, and considering what they were party to, the contractors had no one to complain to. They faced not only huge fines but probably also prison time.

I found out about this through a friend of mine who was a building inspector who was fooled into signing off on some of their work. They would show him a section that was done right, and then finished the job without having him finish the inspecting. When he told them he couldn't sign off on the projects, they tried to bribe him. When he refused, they threatened his family. He fled town to parts unknown and sent me documents, photographs, and recordings he made of the bribe attempts and the threats.

When I was digging a little further into what he sent me, checking addresses and inspection approvals, someone found out. It could have been someone in the planning department who might have been bought off to report anything suspicious. I have more about the people who might have been paid off in the files, but the rot is at the top, with at least two members of the city council on the take in some way.

I don't know how these contractors thought they would get away with it. Not only the criminal behavior, but also what's going to hit them in the next year or so when their houses start coming apart. They're not only crooks, but they're stupid. They must think that getting rid of me will end the threat of exposure, but the houses are still going to fall apart.

Francie, please don't worry about what happened to me. I didn't tell you but I think you knew that my health went south on me a few months ago, in a big, bad way. Not to sound too maudlin, but I kind of thought that if someone did away with me, then my death would accomplish something.

I have faith in you, my dear friend. You are smart enough to get all this out to the right people without becoming a target like I did. If you are going to reveal yourself in any way, make sure they first know that you are protected.

If this seems too dangerous for you, turn it over to Mike Olsen, as this is surely a federal case, and/or to Bogie Spivac, since the crimes have been conducted in his jurisdiction. He could certainly get the ball rolling.

Anyway, I'm fine with leaving with what I was facing. You know my philosophy about coming back on a higher plane. I only wish I could remember where I was and think about you. Blessings upon you, Francie.

He had signed the letter, as he had all his correspondence, with his fountain pen in a custom dark royal blue ink. Her eyes stayed on the letter but her mind ran a slide show of images of her friend, of the site of his death, of his vandalized house. She took a deep breath and let it out slowly through pursed lips. Then she refolded the letter and slipped it into the envelope, putting it on the table. She took the mug, moved the tea bag to a dish on the table, and stirred the brew.

She sat quietly, blowing the steam from over the top of the mug, looking out through the bulletproof glass of the reinforced French doors that opened out onto her deck and beyond, across the open space hard-packed sand and rock dotted with gorse, to the top of her own bluff 75 feet away that dropped 25 feet to the Pacific. The ocean was choppy this day, muffled by a thick haze. Francie's eyes dropped down to the envelope. She sighed again and said aloud, "Time to get to work."

* * * * *

As promised, both the flash drive and the hard drive had the same files. After three hours of scanning most and reading through a number of them, Francie saw how close Douglass had been to finishing his book. She was now settled into the delicious warmth of the hot tub which she thought of as her personal sanctuary. Whether she had had a full day chasing down leads or spent a long time at the computer as she had just done, the hot tub provided physical relief as well as the peace of mind to juggle the information she had absorbed from Douglass' files.

Knowing how he worked, Francie suspected that he had just recently made the queries that brought him the fatal attention. While he didn't name anyone specifically, it didn't require reading between the lines for Francie to realize that the likely villains in the story – at least as far as complicity for financial gain was the issue – were a higher-up in the planning department and two members of the city council.

And that the mayor was involved was a given. Berke Bloom had been voted in because he went to Carmel High, and he displayed a friendly familiarity with many of the citizens who overlooked his frequent intoxication and rudeness to women. He was voted in because the other candidate, who was bright and knew how to handle the impending revenue narrows, had been vice mayor with the previous mayor. While a decent man, the previous mayor had not been a good city leader, and had engendered considerable opprobrium. So the voters in this presumably informed and consciousness community had cast their ballots for Bloom... and against their own and the city's best interests.

Sydnee Loyance had been managing the Carmel planning department for the past three years, since her boss had been on medical leave. After serving in the post for more than 17 years, despite the length of his illness, the city had kept him on the books so he could continue to have medical coverage. Loyance had been effective as his deputy, but her management ability had been wanting. Francie didn't know whether it was the acting manager or someone under her who was most likely responsible for the misprision that caught Douglass' attention. She would see what she could dig up about the woman's personal financial situation later.

As for the council members, there was only one person Francie was sure to be honest, and that was Richie Thurman. Not so Randi Royce who had been appointed by Mayor Bloom to the council seat he had vacated upon his election. No real surprise, since Royce had been manager of Bloom's campaign which had set new lows for truth and decency. Bloom's choice of Royce had been endorsed by Isadora Stramp, the only returning member of the council. Previously she had seemed to keep her head down, but over the past two years, since the election of the new mayor, she had been voting with the mayor and Royce consistently.

The fifth member of the council, Jenna Biss, was another disappointment. Once counted upon for thoughtful participation, she had on a number of recent occasions sided with the "black hats trio."

Francie thought it likely that Douglass had been referring to two council members, not the mayor and a council member. In that case, she thought Royce and Stramp were the most likely, though until she'd done some more research, she wouldn't rule out Biss.

If Francie's view of the Carmel government seemed deleterious, the truth was that most of her Carmel friends and those looking in from the outside shared her negative feelings about the people running the village. They shared a concern that the voters might not awaken to the growing need to vote in competent officials. As one local wag observed, what had happened to Carmel was not unlike what had happened to the nation, and to other democracies around the world... The people had failed in their citizenry duty.

"This is bigger than Trump or the cretinous people running Carmel," Douglass had told Francie when she had visited with him a month earlier. "This is about what has happened to the country. Not only has our school system produced idiots and fools, but the churches have been so politicized, their congregations can no longer distinguish between right and wrong. We're in serious trouble, and I don't know what we might hope for to change our course."

Well, Francie thought as she remembered her friend's comments, at least I can find the people who set up your killing, and take them out of circulation. A darker thought flitted through her mind that maybe they wouldn't make it to court. It disturbed her on two levels to have that thought even get her attention. First, that she could be in danger, something that she hadn't given appropriate consideration to, and second, that she might personally be put in a position of avenging her friend's murder.

Yes, she told herself as she climbed out of the hot tub and wrapped herself in a plush bath sheet. She put the lid down on the tub and went inside the house. She went over in her mind some of her conclusions and directions.

At the top of the list was that she needed to be very careful. She didn't know who might know of her relationship with Douglass, or that he had sent her the information that they had collected from his house.

As those thoughts played through her mind, Francie noticed that her emotional state had shifted from fear to anger, and suddenly vengeance seemed more the route. She also recognized that she didn't want to have these feelings and thoughts. She knew it was possible to eschew the negative, but it took a conscious and deliberate effort to avoid going there. "Yes," she quietly avowed.

*   *   *   *   *

Francie was going to call Mike Olsen and Bogie Spivac anyway, but it was what she discovered in her online search about Sydnee Loyance, the acting planning department manager, and councilwomen Royce and Stramp, that made her pick up the phone. It was a shared pattern of bettering their individual financial situations, specifically improving their lifestyles. They had all moved into upper-scale housing with low-price lease-to-buy options. There was another coincidence that spoke even uglier about the three grifters: the properties were all controlled by a hidden company at the end of a chain of the same five shell companies, though, curiously, not chained in the same order.

"What a surprise," Francie said to the sheriff later that afternoon.

"Aw, Francie," he teased, "just a coincidence."

"Or maybe they just happened to share with each other

their magical connections?" Francie offered.

"Uh-huh."

"And all three of the trails went cold in a bank in Hong Kong."

"Have you talked to Mike about this?"

"I'm calling him next, Bogie. He was on another call when I rang. I wanted to see what your schedule was like so that I can get together with you two."

"Well you're in luck, probably. He and I were supposed to go to a conference in San Jose this evening, but it was postponed until next month. So unless he's moved real fast, we both should be free tonight if that works for you."

"Yes, thanks, Bogie." And she added, "I really like it when the pieces fall into place easily. It says I'm on the right track."

"I just texted Mike. He said how about Tarpy's at 6:30?"

"Grand. Text him I'm buying the wine."

Bogie sounded puzzled when he replied, "But he and I were looking forward to having some Irish whiskey tonight."

"I know. He told me about you two were going to the conference together and about the Irish. Hah. That's why I'm buying the wine."

*   *   *   *   *

It was the middle of the week, so it wasn't difficult to get a table alone in one of the small private rooms off the major dining areas. They had ordered their drinks –

Jameson for the men and an Argentine Malbec for Francie – and some light appetizers. Francie wanted to fully brief them before their entrees arrived, but she needn't have worried about slipping into small talk first. They both had respected and liked Wayne Douglass and whatever they could do to bring his killer or killers to justice, they were all ears.

It took some effort to read Douglass' letter to them without breaking her pace, but they knew her and could hear the strain. When she had finished, Mike patted her arm and Bogie nodded his head sympathetically.

"Okay, that was the tough part. Let me tell you what else I learned, beyond the housing situations of the people Douglass was nailing, when I went online."

Francie went on to tell them of what it appeared they had done to *earn* their condos. It was only inferential, but if it were properly presented in court, a jury would be severely challenged not to find that the prosecution's two-and-two's made four.

"First, there was the favoritism. The Planning Department has tremendous power over what goes on in the village. And since Loyance has been making decisions, people that were personal friends of the mayor got moved to the head of line and were green-lighted with very few questions, while people that were at odds with the mayor ran into one obstacle after another.

"Some of the mayor's closest friends were building and rebuilding around town, something they had held off doing during the previous administration when the procedural waters would have been rougher. While the mayor and his family own a lot of property in Carmel and the surrounding area, the real gold was in making it clear that using contractors that weren't in his good graces was going to take a lot longer, get a lot of inspections, and so cost a lot more. The favoritism generated complaints from those pushed to the back of the line, and from neighbors who said they watched corners being cut. The competing contractors mostly kept their mouths shut, not wanting to have their names wind up on the mayor's blacklist.

"Second, Royce and Stramp have voted with the mayor on every issue. They also publicly endorsed all of his policies as they were presented during public meetings before the council took their vote. I should add that the council meetings have become meaningless from the public's point of view. It used to be that there was discussion by the council members and they heard from the audience, but the black hats on the dais started attacking the public for disagreeing with them."

"And people decided it wasn't worth it to attend?" Mike asked.

Francie nodded. "I can't say that I blame them."

The sheriff raised another issue. "I heard there was a stink last week over a new contract for the city attorney."

"Phew, yes," Francie agreed. "This guy is very close to the mayor. He gave his campaign kick-off speech; it was vile, and full of lies and attacks on decent people. Also, during his tenure he tried to block public access to records that the state says the citizens have a right to see.

He's been sued in court and the judge seemed to think the city attorney was out of line, significantly so."

"And they gave him a new contract anyway?" Mike asked.

Yep," Francie answered. "For five years, and at a rate several times what his predecessor got."

"And they think they can get away with this kind of stuff? Bogie, your office should look into this."

The sheriff nodded.

Mike continued, "And I'll see what I can find out about the Hong Kong connection. Surely it ties into whoever is running the contractors and selling them building materials and whatever."

"Good," said Francie. They had concluded the briefing on the Douglass situation just as the waiter arrived with their main courses. The conversation among the three, friends as well as colleagues, traversed a variety of subjects as they enjoyed their dinners. Invariably one of the topics was their shared concern about the social standards and the stains and tears in them made by individuals who produced their professional challenges.

"I find it disheartening," Francie said, "that fewer people seem to care about the basic rules. Drivers aren't stopping at stop signs. Tourists stand in the middle of the street to take photographs. And pedestrians are three abreast on the sidewalk, making others walk around them. I don't know if it's just a lack of courtesy, or they don't know better. Am I wrong? Weren't people more respectful years back?"

"Yes, they were," the sheriff answered. "I don't know whether it's because of over-population or the culture has changed. Because it's not just the tourists. All sorts of misbehavior is going on. My lieutenants have commented on this. They say the only regrets our deputies are hearing is that they have been caught. The offenders consider themselves victims."

Mike shook his head. "We're seeing a lot of that, too. Is it a plague of narcissism? We arrest people for serious financial crimes, and they seem to think that it isn't fair." And he added. "No wonder people voted for Trump. He's one of them."

"And the scary part is that so many people still support him," Bogie added. "I'm worried for our country."

Francie put in, "I have a feeling the people we're looking at here are of the same mindset."

"I wouldn't be surprised at all," Mike said. "So let's put together an airtight case and let them squeal."

*   *   *   *   *

It was late the next morning that Francie received an email from Mike that linked the Hong Kong bank to LinSing, a large Chinese multinational that was on Interpol's watch list for currency manipulation. There were also issues about the ownership of the company, and if relatives of top Chinese party leaders were sharing in the considerable profits.

The FBI man called not long after sending the email to follow up. "Francie, Bogie and I are agreed that we've got a good paper trail, but we want to flip at least one of the locals to tie a good knot."

Francie chuckled. "I kinda thought we would need to do that. Did you have some member of the august city council in mind?"

"We don't think Biss is corrupt, just on the wrong side. And not the mayor. We want the others to fall on him. So that leaves Loyance in the Planning Department, or Royce and Stramp on the council. Do you have a preference?"

"Hmm. Well, Royce is a hard nut. She might take a lot of work to break. Loyance isn't very bright, but she might shut her mouth and not open it, even if she were offered a good deal."

"Which leaves Isadora Stramp."

"She'd be my choice, Mike. No one has ever accused her of being of strong character. Also, Royce is single – well, her husband is in a care facility and won't be coming out – and Loyance was never married. Stramp is married and has a couple of kids. I think she could be flipped if she knew she was facing a prison term."

"That was our thinking, too. Good. Do you know her? Are you the one to approach her?"

"I don't really know her, but we've met a couple of times at different functions. Yes, I can be the one. Have you and Bogie thought about how you want this to go? Should I shake her up a little with some clues to what's going on and see who she takes it to, maybe Bloom or Royce? Worry the lot of them?"

Later Francie told him that she could almost hear him wince through the phone.

"I suppose that would be the best way, Francie, but you have to be careful. I know I don't have to tell you that. But the mayor and Royce are bad people, not only corrupt but mean. You rattle their cages and they're going to run to their Chinese-funded developer friends. We know what they did to Wayne Douglass."

There was a brief silence before Francie replied. Mike knew to wait. Francie wasn't likely to give a quick response to something that required thought.

"It's funny, Mike, because yes, I'm going to rattle the rats' cages, and yes, they are dangerous, but I want to make sure we put away the people responsible for killing Wayne, even if that means some risk."

"I can't say I'm surprised, Francie, but let us know what you're up to so that we can provide you with all the back-up you need."

"I will, Mike. Thanks."

*   *   *   *   *

"Thank you for meeting with me, Isadora," Francie opened when they had sat down at a table at Carmel Belle. "I know your time is precious."

"Oh, sure, you know. I really think the Park and Recs committee does good work, so when you told me you might have some ideas to help them, that would be great." The woman giggled. "It's really why I like being on the council, you know, so I can run the meetings. I mean, some people just go on and on, you know, and I don't let them go too long."

Isadora Stramp was a heavy woman who had no idea

how to present herself in a better light. Her clothes might have been hand-me-downs from an older sister, her hair needed a trim, at least, and her face lacked the touch of make-up that would have supported her ever-present if somewhat vacuous smile.

"Yes, well, actually, there's something else on my mind. It has to do with a very good friend of mine who died recently." She paused so that the woman might change gears.

Stramp looked confused. "I thought this was about my committee, the Park and Recs committee."

"No, I told you that because I felt it was important to speak to you privately, not after a council or committee meeting."

"Oh. So, what did you want to talk to me about?" Then she remembered. "Your friend who died?"

"Yes, you knew him. Wayne Douglass." Francie could see in that moment as the councilwoman took it in that she did know him, but she made no connection to her own situation. But she was about to.

"I think you probably heard that he had died."

She nodded her head. "Uh-huh, yes I read about it in the *Pine Cone*, I think. He fell off a cliff or something."

"Actually, he didn't fall, Isadora," Francie corrected, and then dropped the bomb. "He was murdered."

Stramp's mouth dropped open with surprise. Murder wasn't part of her life. Or so she had thought.

"Douglass was preparing to publish a book. That's why

he was killed."

She clasped her hands over her bosom. "Oh my goodness. How terrible."

"It gets worse," Francie warned her. And followed with, "And you figured in his book, rather prominently."

"Me? I'm in his book? Oh really?" Still confused, that she was going to be in someone's book.

"It's not a novel. It's a well-evidenced report on corruption here in the Carmel government. That's why he was murdered."

Slowly a realization began to seep into her consciousness. Her breathing became shallow.

Francie continued. "The killers stole the manuscript and the folders of notes that he had worked from."

There might have been a flicker of relief or hope that flashed across her eyes, but it was quickly dashed.

"But Douglass knew that his book would send a number of people to prison – public officials who had been involved in the corruption. He knew he was in danger. That's why the day he was struck down and pushed off the bluff, he FedEx'd a copy of his manuscript and all of his notes and evidence to someone he knew that would publish the book for him."

Francie waited until the silence was too long for the woman to look away. Finally, when Stramp's eyes rose to meet hers, Francie said, "He sent the files to me, Isadora, because he and I were good friends, and he knew I would get his book published."

"Oh my god," the woman protested, her voice rising. "I didn't know anything. I didn't know." Terror was written all over her face. It appeared that she didn't know whether to scream or run, but she was too frozen to do either.

Francie watched fear and chaos play across her face. Her shoulders were shaking and her hands were clasped so tightly before her on the table that her knuckles were white. Soon her breathing moved back toward normal, and Francie set the hook.

"Why did you do it, Isadora? Did you really think you could get away with taking that money?"

The woman tried to speak but she couldn't find any words that might match her thoughts in an exculpatory manner.

Francie leaned slightly forward. "Listen to me, I don't think you ever imagined that the people you were tied to – the mayor, Randi Royce, and the others – would ever commit murder."

Stramp shook her head, both in shock and denial.

"So here's the situation. If you tell the authorities everything you know, everything you did, and everyone who was involved, then they will tell the district attorney – and the U.S. attorney – that you didn't realize what you had gotten into and you agree to come clean."

The wheels were turning in the woman's mind but they were going in different directions. Not surprisingly, Francie thought, considering how her world had suddenly come crashing down around her. She let her have a little more time and then broke through the disorder.

"I know this is sudden, but you have to pull yourself together. You need to realize that not only will you face corruption and IRS charges, but you could be charged as an accessory to murder."

If she had been shocked before, Isadora Stramp was close to sliding out of her chair.

"It all depends on whether you're smart enough to save yourself. The sooner you act, the better off you will be. I can tell you this, there's a big difference between being locked up in the federal prison in Dublin off of highway 680, or the state prison down south in Chowchilla."

"How...? Wha...? Oh my god." She placed her hands over her face. Her shoulders shook as she silently sobbed.

Francie waited. Finally the sobs stopped and Stramp sat up. She took a handkerchief from a pocket, sniffed, and wiped the tears from her face.

"I know you feel like the sky has fallen in on you, and it has. You're in serious trouble, but you know what?" She stopped there until the woman was looking at her again, her expression a mixture of despair, and maybe now some hope?

"You'll get through this. Despite the trust that you have betrayed, you'll survive. Wayne Douglass was a very good man. Honest and bright. And he was murdered to prevent you and your associates from having to face the law. You can't bring him back, but you can bring him justice."

Francie stood up and said, "If you have any sense, you'll save your own situation. Understand?"

Stramp nodded her head slowly, though not enthusias-tically. Francie rested her hands palms down on the table halfway to the woman, and then she leaned forward. "This shouldn't be complicated for you. You have twenty-four hours." She looked up at a clock on the wall. "I'll be back here are at 10:45 tomorrow morning. If you're not here, you'll have the FBI knocking on your door by lunchtime. Is that clear?"

The nodding became vigorous and the woman moaned. Francie stood back up, looked at the misery she had produced, turned to walk away.

*   *   *   *   *

Francie knew from the moment she pushed away from the table that Stramp's reaction was wrong. The council-woman was not in a sorrowful woe-is-me frame of mind. Her expression was anticipation. What she was antici-pating Francie could only imagine. What Francie knew was that Stramp was a better actress than she had given her credit for. It meant that Francie had probably been set up, that the woman had a microphone on her or in her bag. And that Francie could expect company either when she walked out onto San Carlos Street, or maybe when she got into her car.

But she and her law enforcement colleagues had consid-ered this possibility. She peered forward, searching for something amiss; there was nothing visible. Francie turned a 180 and with her right hand pulled her Glock 19 from the holster on the back of her belt. As she swung it around in front of her, her left had met the gun and pulled back the slide, loading a 9mm bullet into the chamber. Then her left hand went up to her face, her forefinger on her lips telling Stramp to be silent.

But the silence was shattered behind her out on the street with screams of alarm and five shots fired quickly, by two different guns. Francie was tempted to turn around and see what had happened but she wasn't going to take her eyes off the woman who had fooled her until the last moment.

And the proof of Francie's new wisdom was that this time when Isadora Stramp froze, her face portrayed not confusion but hatred. She understood that her act hadn't worked, that any expectation that Francie would be removed from the playing field now was history.

Francie's finger had come down from her face. She pointed at the table. "Arms out," she ordered. "Reach across the table with both hands and hope I won't shoot you for killing my friend."

That message got through. The woman smoothly reached as far as she could across the table, her head on its side, her face pointing away and slightly back.

"Francie!" called the familiar voice of Sheriff Spivac. He was standing slightly behind a wooden pillar and not moving, just in case something spooked her.

Without turning around, she called out "Bogie!" and with obvious relief. "I haven't searched her so I can't come out yet. What happened outside? Are you and your people all right?"

"Me and mine are all fine. They had three young men, Chinese, waiting for you. They were sitting at a table near the door, listening in on one of their phones. She must be wearing a wire of some sort."

"What went down?"

There was a pause. Then the sheriff said with a sigh. "They all drew on us. They all went down." His tone changed, "Francie, I'm sending a couple of deputies in, one this way and one through the Ocean Avenue entrance. Those areas were both being watched. They'll take the prisoner. You're good."

"Thank you," – she was about to call him by his nick-name again but this time she caught herself – "Sheriff."

She had never taken her eyes off her prisoner and didn't until the deputies had come in a few seconds later, and not very gently cuffed her behind her back. They were about to lead her away when Francie told them to stop.

"Wait. Bend her over the table and give her a thorough, skin-level search. She may have a bug on her. Make it very close. It maybe something like a small wafer. Remove any jewelry. I'll go through her bag."

Councilwoman Stramp was then bent over, emitting an involuntary "Ooof!" as she was tabled. Francie tried to hide the smile it brought to her vengeful mind. She carefully emptied the contents of the bag onto another table. Nothing she didn't expect. No weapons, but her cellphone was on a call, no doubt to the people outside. She asked the deputies to note the status of the phone, which they did. She doubted their testimony was going to be required in a court, considering all the charges that the councilwoman would be facing, and would plead down to.

"Nothing, ma'am." The deputies had done their body search quickly and professionally. The suspect was stood up from the table, the deputies took the woman's bag into which Francie had restored all of the contents, and then led her out to the Ocean Avenue entrance.

Francie walked out toward San Carlos and saw teams of EMTs standing by two covered bodies and another putting the lone survivor in an awaiting ambulance. Just as they were closing the doors on the vehicle, one of the medicos looked over at the sheriff and gave him a thumbs up.

"Good," the sheriff said aloud and Francie came up to him. "One of the men who was shot looks like he'll survive. Maybe we can find out what happened." He had an artificial look of hope on his face, which was underscored as he raised his eyebrows. He said quietly, "I'm pretty sure they're from one of the new Bay Area Tong gangs. They have their own tattoos. They're nasty, worse than the Russian mafia. They have their own internecine battles, but they also hire themselves out for hits, here, on the North Coast, and down the Central Valley past Fresno."

"Lovely to see young people with gainful employment."

"Yep."

"No word yet from Mike on Bloom and Loyance?"

He held his hand to the bud in his ear. He listened briefly and then spoke quietly but distinctly into a microphone on a cord hanging around his neck. "Got it, Mike. Get 'em booked. The DA wants us to meet at his office tomorrow morning at ten. That will give the different jurisdictions time to handle the booking, and his office time to get caught up on what we have.

Security in the lobby has been notified that we'll be coming in."

He listened again, said, "Right. Francie will brief Ed and whoever he assigns to the case." Another pause, and then. "Right. See you tomorrow."

Then he said to Francie, "Okay, you know the situation. Everyone's been picked up and are being booked. We'll take care of your capture, and Mike will get Royce, Loyance, and Bloom."

Francie chuckled. "Sounds like a law firm, doesn't it?"

"Or in this case, an unlaw firm."

They laughed, not loudly.

"It was very smart of you, Francie, checking with the Monterey tower, asking them to let us know if anyone filed a new flight plan. They called about a half-hour ago, around the time you were sitting down with the Stramp woman. A long-distance Gulfstream at the Jet Center filed for a departure to San Diego, wheels up in twenty minutes. Bloom must have been spooked when he heard from Stramp that you wanted to talk to her. He wouldn't have bought it that you wanted to talk about Park and Recs. He decided to skedaddle with Loyance, with whom, as I told you, he was having an affair. Anyway, Mike was waiting for them when they drove up at the Jet Center. The flight crew had been on stand-by, and the plane had been fueled and pre-flighted, and ready to go, but they weren't going anywhere."

"The aircraft's and crew's flight logs should be checked, too, Bogie. There may be a clue to if they flew people in here, or maybe to Santa Rosa, around the time Wayne was murdered."

"We will check that out, France, but I have to think, considering who we had down here, that whoever was giving the orders would have gotten people like these from San Francisco."

France nodded her considered agreement. But suddenly she stopped. "Maybe the killings, yes, but maybe they needed someone smarter to look through Wayne's house. I mean, it's hardly likely that these people would have known what to look for."

"I think you're right. And that would explain why they didn't go to the house that night." He rubbed his chin. "Have a favorite who might have done the break-in?"

"Of the crowd we know?"

"They would have the best knowledge of what to look for."

"Yes," she said, and her tone of voice impelled the sheriff to follow her eyes. They had reached his car, but it was the car behind it that had garnered her attention. It looked very much like an unmarked police car, which it was. And because they were close enough, they could see through the tinted windows. Francie was looking at Randi Royce in the back seat, propped forward because she was handcuffed behind her back.

"Ah, I see what you mean. She would by far be the likeliest to have known what to look for in his house, and from what we know of her, she would have taken pleasure in messing up the house."

"Messing it up after she had packed up the files and his

computer. Adding insult to injury."

"Bogie, can I be with you when you interrogate her?"

"Sure."

She thought some more. "One of the things we need to find out is who coordinated with Stramp to have the call to the men outside. Someone had to set that up. I called yesterday morning to set up the meeting, which would have explained Bloom's making sure that the plane was ready to leave this morning, but I don't see him as the one to call in a hit squad. More like he would just leave Stramp out to dry."

"You're thinking it would be Royce again, aren't you? That she would have the connections, probably up to whoever was the money behind this whole thing."

"Yes. That could be why she got behind Bloom's mayoral campaign. She could run him with both hands tied behind her back." She laughed as she looked back at the car in which she was stashed. "So to speak," she affirmed.

"What a witch," he commented looking back at the woman who remained bent over in the back of the car.

"Did she give your people any trouble?" she asked.

The Sheriff cocked his head across the street at the Wells Fargo bank. "She was over there, maybe wanting to watch the fireworks. But as soon as the first shot was fired, she headed for the back door of the bank. My people had been following her since she left her house this morning. They had no trouble with her. They're going to take her over to the Monterey office for booking and keep her there overnight since they want her at the DA's office in the morning. You want to be with us for the booking?"

"No thanks, my friend," she said, taking out her phone. "I'll check with Ed and find out if he wants me to come over now and get them up to speed on what we know. I think he'll say yes." She shook her head.

"What is it?"

"I think I'll get a walk in by the ocean this afternoon. I feel sullied having been with that woman this morning."

"I can understand that."

"Also, it's unnerving to have taken my gun out. I mean, I was right and handled it all professionally, but if for a moment I thought she was responsible for Wayne's death, or knew of it before it happened...I guess I don't know. It's something I have to work through."

The sheriff put his large hand on Francie's shoulder and gave it a long, gentle squeeze. "Francie, first of all, I've never known you to even approach doing something like that. There was that bastard at the college who killed the professor, and he had a knife, but that's not who you are. In fact, I'm surprised you're even thinking such thoughts. But I do think a walk by the ocean would be a wonderful idea. And call me if you need anything. Anytime, you know that."

She wanted to give her friend a hug, but not in public, so she just gave him a deep smile, and walked down the street. When she got to her car, she called the DA's office and was quickly put through to the man in charge, Ed Pollito, who had been the district attorney of Monterey

County for five terms.

"Hello, Francie," he said in a boisterous voice. "I hear you're wiping out crime in my jurisdiction. Thanks for the work you're giving us."

Francie laughed. "Hi, Ed. Glad to do my bit. Especially as this ties in with the murder of Wayne Douglass, who was a good friend of mine."

"So I heard from the sheriff. Yes, I'm sorry. Okay, I'd like you to come in and tell me and my people everything we should know about what happened, who we're dealing with, and what kind of evidence you have. The sheriff says you've got a lot of information."

"I do, Ed. I can come by now or whenever you like."

"Now would be great. I imagine you might be hungry. I'll get some lunch laid out for you."

"You're a prince, Ed, thanks. See you in about fifteen minutes."

       *   *   *   *   *

When Francie arrived at the Monterey court building, she told one of the guards at the security check point that the district attorney was expecting her and showed her ID. The guard said she needed to go through the scanner.

"I thought they had called down to clear me. I'm carrying a Glock 19 on the back of my belt," Francie told her. "I have a concealed weapons permit and just participated in a bust of several violent offenders with Sheriff Spivac along with the FBI. I'll show you my weapon and my permit if you want to see it, but I'm not going inside if I have to give it up."

At that moment a woman Francie recognized as the DA's chief administrative assistant came hurriedly down the stairs. She called out to the guard, "Esther, this woman is one of the white hats. She's with me."

The guard looked at one of the other guards who shrugged. "All right, Lannie. I guess you can bend the rules, since you're the one who wrote 'em."

The woman laughed. "Thank you, Esther." With that, she took Francie's elbow and guided her out of the security area. "Sorry about that," she said to Francie. "I got stuck on the phone."

"And I made better time than I thought getting here. All's well. Thank you."

Lannie brought her over to the elevators where one stood open as if waiting for them. Francie would have preferred the stairs, to work off her extra energy, but she didn't want to make a fuss. She rode up with the woman to the top floor, and went with her to the conference room. At a side table were sandwiches, side dishes, and a variety of drinks.

"Do you have your own caterer on site?"

"Hah. We do this every week for our regular top staff meeting. Saves time for people going out for lunch."

"Smart."

"And the food is good. Francie, Mr. Pollito asks that you fix yourself a feast and take a seat at the end of the table," she said pointing. "He'll be in with Jeannie Irish and Marc Arbovitz in just a few minutes. Oh, and don't wait for them to have your lunch. He was emphatic about that."

Francie laughed. "Thank you, Lannie. I can't imagine how this office would work without you."

The woman laughed brightly again. "Oh, please. But thank you," she said with an appreciative smile. "Find me if you don't see what you want."

"Will do," Francie said, as the woman left. She looked at the food and suddenly realized how hungry she was. It had been an eventful morning. Imagine, she thought, if her realization of Stramp's anticipation hadn't kicked in. She chuckled to herself, remembering that she wanted to let herself off the hook from any errors she corrected before they took effect. She took a plate and selected what she wanted for lunch. Then, as directed, she took a seat at the end of the table and began on her sandwich.

Her timing had been good, if unintentional. She had all but finished her lunch by the time, not many minutes later, that Ed and his two top prosecutors came into the conference room. There were introductions, and then Francie suggested they get lunch and she would tell them what they needed to know while they ate. Then they could ask follow-up questions. They agreed, and with pens unsheathed and yellow pads next to their food they listened, ate, and took notes. They all had their fill of food and information in less than an hour. The district attorney congratulated Francie on cracking the case, and asked her to forward copies of Douglass' files when she was back at her desk.

*   *   *   *   *

Francie stopped on the way home, parking in the lot by the little red Bay School at the north end of Monastery Beach. The school had seemed closed for years, its parking area enjoyed by those who walked to and on the dirt service road above the beach between Carmel Meadows and South Carmel Bay. The road ran to the mouth of the Carmel River and was used by the state parks people for picking up the trash after weekends and holidays. Mostly it was greatly enjoyed by the people who walked it, between the well-tended yards plush with flora stretching down from the pricey houses above, and the grasses, wild roses, California poppies, and fragrant alyssum growing on the ocean side.

Francie kept a pair of walking shoes behind the front seat of her car to take advantage of this restorative walk when she returned from a business meeting on The Peninsula that called for more fashionable footwear. In two minutes, she had walked past the stand of redolent eucalyptus trees onto the road. It was a liberating moment from all the cares of the day, particularly this day which connected the oft-shared poles of violence and victory.

With an extraordinarily serene vista before her, Francie saw in her mind's eye the ugly anger of the exposed Isadora Stramp, the black-bagged bodies of two men she didn't know who had come to kill her, and the smiling face of Wayne Douglass, who had brought it all to her. "Almost done, Wayne," she said aloud. Had someone been walking toward her at that moment, they might have noticed the glistening of sorrow in her eyes.

*   *   *   *   *

Francie woke up shortly after seven the next morning, later than usual. Not that she was pressed, but she noted that she had slept unusually soundly. She felt particularly well rested, couldn't remember any of her dreams, and the bed clothes were less mussed than usual. Sleep was an important issue for her. She never scheduled anything early in the morning that she might have to use an alarm clock, and she kept her cellphone in her office so its dings connoting incoming emails and messages or news breaks wouldn't bother her. If someone needed to reach her, her special phone line would ring on her desk twenty feet away, and only three people had that number: Bogie Spivac, Mike Olsen, and Ariane Chevasse, her best friend and frequent collaborator.

Ariane was a wizard with electronics and when it came to security, there was none better, which was why government agencies were constantly calling for her consulting expertise. And why Francie's house had one of the best private security systems on the West Coast. In addition to her technical expertise – and because of it – Ariane had access to some of the highest levels of national and global security information. Which was why, after she had showered and dressed and had her first cup of her new Illy coffee – a gift from her friend and occasional client, the hotelier Denny LeVett – Francie had called Ariane.

"*Bon jour, chère amie,*" said the warm voice of her Francophile friend. "I think you were involved in the event in Carmel yesterday."

Francie laughed. "You have such a suspicious mind, my friend. But yes, I was there."

"Geoffrey and I were camping in Big Sur the last two days, mercifully out of touch with this mad world. We got back late last night, that is when I found out about what happened. I knew you were all right, so I would call you this morning. Would you fill me in, please?"

And Francie did. She had already apprised her of the situation at The Sea Ranch and what Douglass' files had revealed. Ariane's sources had informed her of the official report of what had happened the day before, but Francie wove through that her personal experience.

"You were the heroine again, Francie," Ariane said, pride in her voice. "Your intuition is so powerful."

"It does play an ever more important role, doesn't it?"

"*Mais oui*, but most people don't know that it needs to be cultivated."

"Or they don't want to bother," Francie replied.

"So, you asked me to find out about LinSing. I found out some very interesting points."

"I thought you might, my wonderful spook friend."

They laughed together.

"First of all, LinSing has earned serious attention from all the major international law enforcement agencies. In part because they are tight with the Xi regime. He may have made himself the leader-for-life, but associations with conglomerates like LinSing may cut his term down. They have too many subsidiaries and affiliations, and some of those subsets are involved in drugs and human trafficking. Mostly that is overlooked by the top company officials – they don't want to know – because they are greedy, and because they don't want to be blamed. So they can deny having known what the people below them have done. Are doing."

"I imagine there are operations like that in many countries."

"*Bien sûr, cherie.* Guns and money, money and guns. Some day we will make better choices."

"From your lips to god's ears."

"Maybe when god is a woman."

There was a short silence, and then Francie asked, "Anything on Randi Royce?"

"Hah! You will love this." And for several minutes, Ariane told Francie what she had learned about this village councilwoman. When she was finished, she invited Francie to come over for dinner that night. When she happily agreed to the invitation and hung up the phone, Francie called the Sheriff with a request.

*   *   *   *   *

Ed Pollito sat at the head of the table with his top assistants, Jeannie Irish and Marc Arbovitz flanking him. Mike Olsen and the sheriff were on one side of the table and Francie was on the other.

"Thank you for coming here this morning," the district attorney began. "And thank you for your excellent work. I can't remember when we have had such a convoluted case involving such a small community as you have brought to us. Are there any updates to what we received from you yesterday?" From the expression on his face and his posture, it was clear that neither he nor his associates had any idea what was coming.

"Actually, Ed, there are," said Sheriff Spivac, which sent three sets of eyebrows higher. "First, let me catch you up on the shooter in the hospital. We've had an interpreter with him since he regained consciousness. However, he hasn't said a word, no surprise, and apparently his condition is worsening. He probably won't last out the next 48 hours."

"That's too bad," the DA commented.

"Yes, but our initial intel on him and the two others is that they were members of Gung Fu, one of the new Tong gangs to spring up in the Bay Area. They are fanatical, frighteningly so, and have never been known to break their trust with the gang. They know their families would be tortured and killed if they did, and families are all important. The gang is their first family.

"Also, none of the three had anything identifying on them but a single tattoo, which put them in that Tong."

"What was the tattoo?" Marc Arbovitz asked.

The sheriff paused for effect and then said, "It was a dragon with a skeleton head."

"Charming," came the assistant's caustic response.

"They had no credit cards or driver licenses. Just a few hundred dollars each in cash. And the labels were cut out of their clothes. We confirmed their identities with fingerprints and DNA. I should also tell you that the SFPD were most cooperative, and they thanked us for taking these three down. Unfortunately, there are an estimated seventy known members of the Gung Fu gang."

"Good lord," said Pollito, looking at the woman beside him. "Another reason not to go to San Francisco, huh, Jeannie?"

She nodded her head.

"Anything else, Sheriff?"

"Yes, Ed. It's about Randi Royce. She's been booked on a no-bail charge of accessory to attempted murder, but more information has come to light about her, and we want her held incommunicado for reasons that will come clear shortly."

"That's why you asked me to postpone our meeting for an hour?"

"Yes, Ed."

The DA exchanged glances with his two assistants. "Go ahead."

"Since Francie came to Mike and me with the information she'd received from Wayne Douglass, sent to her on the day he was murdered, and that she has forwarded to you..." He waited the moment for confirming nods from the three at the end of the table. "We've been wondering who were the brains behind his murder. The Tong people, who we believed actually killed him, were certainly acting under someone else's orders." He cleared his throat.

"The game was to enable developers to make large sums of money by building and renovating high-priced houses using shoddy materials and sub-standard workmanship. This was enabled by the city Planning

Department that approved the blueprints and theoretically oversaw the work. I say developers but there was actually one firm behind this using different contractors who were supplied by companies all under the same roof.

"As noted in the information that Francie got from Douglass, these suppliers were the same firms that were previously reported to have supplied the toxic trailers supplied to FEMA to house the people made homeless when Hurricane Katrina hit New Orleans. These same suppliers, through shell companies with other names, were found to have shipped the rotten wallboard to a number of high-end housing projects on the Florida Gulf Coast.

"We think there were situations throughout the Central Coast, especially in Pebble Beach, where some of the same contractors built homes using materials from the same suppliers. But for the purposes of our investigation based on Douglass' research, the people who made this happen in Carmel were Sydney Loyance, the woman running the Planning Department for the past three years; the Mayor, Berke Bloom, who kept her in what was supposed to be a temporary position; and council members Randi Royce and Isadora Stramp who not only twice ratified Loyance's appointment but also backed Bloom in passing council actions that made it easier for contractors approved by the Planning Department to build without the normal timeline requirements and safety inspections."

Pollito checked with both of his assistants as he said, "I think we have all of this, don't we?" They nodded their agreement.

"Right," said the sheriff. "Of these four people, we found plenty of greed to go around, but only one person with the guile to plan and manage the scheme." He paused briefly, and then told them, "Randi Royce."

"The rest took orders from her?" Marc asked.

"Indirectly. Royce, you will remember, ran Bloom's mayoral campaign and then he put her on the city council...at her suggestion. He acquiesced, even though he knew it could look bad because he thought she had done such a good job of getting him elected. In truth, she didn't have to work very hard because many in the town were fed up with his predecessor and the previous vice mayor. Plus, Bloom was well-known around town.

"Anyway, she was the power behind the throne. She explained to Bloom what needed to be done by the Planning Department to ease regulations to make his contractor friends happy, and he was happy to implement her suggestions. Especially when the contractors, knowing which side of their bread was buttered, lavished their appreciation on Bloom. Loyance was also well taken care of though Bloom didn't know about that until later. He didn't know that Royce was getting paid off, too, but it wouldn't have surprised, or bothered, him.

"With Royce pulling the strings, the mayor easily brought Stramp into the fold. Stramp's husband had lost his job with the county, and they were being squeezed financially. They were delighted to be given a larger house to live in and rent-free, by an anonymous benefactor."

"You have proof of all this, Sheriff?" asked an incredulous Jeannie Irish.

"Yes we do. After we booked Bloom and Loyance on suspicion of RICO violations, we spoke with them separately. First, Loyance. At this point they didn't know about the shooting on San Carlos, and when we informed her that she would be charged with accessory to attempted murder, she broke down and sang like a lark. She said she had nothing to do with any violence, insisting that everything she did she thought was legal because she said it was authorized by the mayor."

The sheriff smiled. "Next we talked to Bloom, who initially pretended ignorance of anything illegal. Then we confronted him with what we had from Douglass' research. He became itchy but was still resistant, claiming he didn't really know what happened in the Planning Department, and he just had a personal – cough, cough – relationship with Loyance. When we told him of her confession he turned white. I thought he was going to faint. After a glass of water, he spilled the beans, on both Royce, who he blamed for getting him into this, and Stramp whom he described as stupid and greedy.

"What we got from Bloom certainly cemented our conclusion that Royce was the brains behind all of this, both the political and the financial. When we invited her to talk, she gave us a blank look and said she had nothing to say. Just that she'd been in her bank depositing her meager – as she put it – paycheck for her work on the council, and when she went to leave, she was suddenly arrested. She had no idea what murder she was thought to have attempted, or why she shouldn't have been allowed to call her lawyer.

"When we told her of the statements made by Loyance and Bloom, she looked amazed. She even laughed at our investigator, asking if this was some sort of macabre joke, which, she said, wasn't very funny. Then she just shut down and refused to say anything.

"Then this morning we learned more about Royce's background. Apparently she is one of a number of agents embedded in state and city governments by a foreign power."

"China?" asked Pollito.

"Yes, though not directly by the Xi government. By a faction in a large Chinese conglomerate working in association with a clique within his government. We don't know if it was with his knowledge or perhaps was a rogue operation."

"This is like what the Russians were doing in the 2016 election," the DA put in.

"Something like that. Yes, their aim was to create divisions in government bodies, ultimately undermining Americans' faith in their leaders. That was Russia's intention. The Chinese situation was more about providing markets for some of their crony construction manufacturers."

The DA scoffed. "Some communists. They should call themselves Capitalist China." The remark provoked snickers from his assistants. He got serious again, and leaning forward he asked, "But how did Royce fit into all of this?"

"One of the companies that was part of this conglomerate is LinSing. It was banned by the State Department two years ago for corrupt practices, but earlier this year, Trump rescinded the order, saying they had cleaned up their act. They hadn't, but from what we were told, it was in order to get Chinese government support to build three Trump resorts in Beijing, Shanghai, and Hong Kong."

"Holy Hannah!" The DA's comment briefly stopped the conversation. "Sorry. Go ahead."

"Royce was an agent of LinSing. Her job was exactly what she did. Corrupt the city government of the village, probably as a practice run for her or for other agents, and to help other companies in the same conglomerate to sell their sub-standard building materials at inflated prices, and in a way that the poor quality wouldn't become apparent for a few years. By which time, she would have left the scene."

Jeannie Irish asked, "But how did she become involved with a Chinese plot against her own country?"

The sheriff smiled, looked over at Francie, who smiled back, and then answered. "That's what had us wondering, too. But we found out this morning that she was here on false papers. She was born in China, the daughter of a woman high-up in the Chinese Central Committee and an American general who was attached to the embassy in what was then Peking. The man was recalled by Washington, and the child was raised to hate America. She was trained from an early age to be an agent against the United States, and even went so far as to have surgery done on her face, especially her eyes, so that she might pass without question as a Caucasian. She came in through New York from London five years ago and moved out here three years ago."

The silence that followed lasted for almost thirty seconds, when Ed Pollito, shaking his head declared, "This is incredible. Absolutely incredible, and in so many ways. Yes, the corruption in our local government and the collusion – if I can use that word – with the Chinese building suppliers. But also that this should be part of an international conspiracy, right here in our own Monterey County." He shook his head, despairingly. "What do you want us to do with her?"

"We're going to talk to the State Department at some point. I'll let you know where that leads us."

"Very good." The DA stood up, his assistants rising with him. "Well done, all of you. You are a credit to the very principles of justice, and on behalf of the county, I thank you."

*   *   *   *   *

What wasn't mentioned at the meeting with the District Attorney was the conversation that Francie had with Randi Royce earlier that morning at the sheriff's lock-up. It would have been hard to describe it. It had been hard for Mike Olsen and Sheriff Spivac to watch it through a two-way mirror, anxious for Francie as the woman she was talking to in a reasoned tone virtually exploded when confronted with new evidence against her.

It began with Francie entering the room where Royce sat on a bench behind a table, both bolted to the floor. Royce was handcuffed and the cuffs were attached to a chain around her waist; she was also shackled at the ankles. Francie introduced herself. Royce remained silent. Francie explained that her reason for being there was to determine who had killed her friend, Wayne Douglass. Royce again said nothing.

"You have an insurmountable problem, Ms. Royce," Francie said evenly, "Your confederates have all flipped on you. What makes your situation even more tenuous is that you are clearly the only one with the intelligence and wile to put this all together."

The woman was taking in what Francie was saying but seemed to think she didn't have to answer.

Francie smiled. "I think you are expecting us to turn you over to the State Department, and they will arrange to exchange you, quietly, for an American who has gotten into trouble in China." That caused a flicker in the woman's eyes.

"Unfortunately for you," she continued, "the State Department is unlikely to ship you out with a murder charge hanging over your head."

She suddenly spat out, "I didn't murder anyone."

Francie's smile was gone. "Apparently you're not familiar with the law in California, Ms. Royce. If you are party to a murder, even if you weren't present at the scene of the killing, you can be charged with the full crime. That means when you told your handlers that Wayne Douglass had information that was going to blow up your Carmel game, you were as guilty as if you'd killed him yourself."

"I didn't call anyone. I didn't know about that."

"But you must have known, since you were up at his house two days later, taking his laptop and his files...and then trashing the man's home. How vulgar of you."

The comment netted an attempt at a smirk, and then the woman insisted, "I wasn't at his house."

Francie feigned surprise. "Really? You were not only seen by the concierge when you asked for directions..."

"I never was at the lodge. I didn't ask for directions."

"What lodge?"

That shook up the woman. "I wasn't there," she said, now angry with herself for falling into Francie's trap.

"But you were, and you were caught by two security cameras that my friend had set up outside the house. The video shows you clearly through the windows both by his desk and upstairs when you tore his clothes apart. Was that really necessary?"

The woman was now rocking herself back and forth slightly, trying to calm herself down.

"Anyway," Francie said easily. "All that doesn't matter. They have your cellphone call the night before you were arrested, the one that brought those three killers down to Carmel, ostensibly to take me out of the picture."

"You can't have such a call since I didn't make it."

"Oh, I don't mean on your personal phone," Francie quickly explained. "It was your special phone. The throw-away phone. You see, the cell towers record every call on every system. And we were watching all of the calls out of this area starting the moment Isadora

Stramp called Berke Bloom to tell him of her plan to meet with me the next morning."

That painted concern across the woman's face. Then as quickly as it appeared, it dissolved into a sneer.

Francie gave her a moment's feeling of victory and then told her, "We don't have to prove it was your phone. The trace places in the exact spot you were when you made the call. And because you were being followed, we have two witnesses to your exact GPS location."

The sneer slowly ebbed from her face.

"I don't have anything to say to you. I want to speak to my lawyer."

Francie shook her head. "I don't think so."

"What do you mean?" she demanded angrily.

Francie dropped her own mask and simply peered at the woman for a very long minute. Then she reached into her jacket pocket and pulled out a piece of paper, folded into the size of a business card. She opened it up and then placed it on the table before her, her hand covering it, ready to push it across the table.

"This is why they will never take you back." Then she slid the paper to in front of the woman and uncovered it with her hand.

Royce had been staring at Francie, trying to intimidate her by looking into her eyes but she couldn't hold it. Her eyes went down to the piece of paper and immediately widened. She let out a scream and then in a fury tried to stand up and reach for Francie, but the chains holding her hands to her waist and the shackles on her ankles resulted in her falling off the bench and onto the floor. Seconds later, Mike and Bogie were in the room standing over the woman now moaning and crying on the floor.

A deputy came in through another door and looked down at the woman and back up to the sheriff. The sheriff looked at Francie who had remained seated. "I think you're finished with her, yes?"

Francie nodded. "Yes, she's done."

"Get a second person, put her cuffs on her back, and take her back to her cell," the Sheriff instructed the deputy. "Check medical to see whether she needs to be sedated. And make sure there's a 24-hour watch on her. We don't know what she is capable of. She's dangerous and could be a threat to herself as well as others."

*   *   *   *   *

Francie and Mike sat in front of the sheriff's desk as Bogie poured Jameson into three glasses. "We should be drinking this before going to the DA's office?" she asked. Answering the question herself, she raised her glass in the air, the two men clinked their glasses against hers, and the three of them took a long sip of the amber liquid.

"Jesus, France," said Mike, "Did you know how she would react when you showed her that?"

Francie shook her head. "I thought it could go one or two ways. Either she would collapse or she would explode. That's why I asked Bogie to make sure she couldn't get at me if it was the latter."

"Thank goodness," he replied.

"Thank Ariane for coming up with the idea. She was right how much Royce obsessed against the United States, and particularly her own genes. She emailed to me the symbols of her father's name in Chinese." She sighed. "I didn't know if I would have to use it, and what it would produce, but I think we got our answer. Ariane said if the truth about her father being an American got out, Beijing would deny her completely. They knew, of course, but the shame of it going public would be unacceptable to them."

"It was brilliant, Francie," Bogie said. "Tell Ariane we owe her a big dinner."

Francie smiled and finished off the Jameson in her glass. "I wish we didn't have to go over and see Ed now. I could sit sipping this stuff with you guys the rest of the day."

Mike finished his drink and put his glass down on the desk. "We can't tell him what happened, what she said, right?"

Bogie looked at Francie who peered off into that space where answers could sometimes be found. After a moment she took a deep breath and let it out.

"I don't think so," she said. "This will be a case for the Sonoma County district attorney. Besides, I think she's a broken woman, now with no home. I think it will take some time, maybe a couple of days, but she being a smart woman will decide to make the best of a terrible situation and tell you what she knows. I think this is going to remain local. She'll have to plead. If she doesn't take fifteen years, I'll be in court telling the sentencing judge how Wayne Douglass was such a fine, noble man and a good friend."

*   *   *   *   *

Francie asked Mike and Bogie if the three of them might get together for dinner again, this time to get some closure on the case. One or the other of them had other engagements for the next few days, but their schedules meshed on the following Sunday. Francie suggested that they come to her house, and promised to have some Jameson. It wasn't required to seal the deal, but it was certainly appreciated.

In addition to picking up the whiskey and some Sierra Nevada to go with the meal she planned, Francie went down the Valley to Baja Cantina for a special order of ribs, chicken, coleslaw, and beans. Plus, of course, their renowned chips and salsa.

"I do love the food at Chez Francie," Bogie commented, as they ate their way through the feast she had laid out for them.

"She's gonna get another Michelin star one of these days," Mike put in. "But don't tell anyone, Francie. The crowds would have your neighbors boiling tar and plucking feathers."

"You're the only stars I want here," said the clever object of their appreciation.

"Aw, shucks, Francie."

"Yeah, Mike, but she's right. We don't want to share her with anyone, do we?"

"No one we know, at any rate."

"You guys...." she replied and they all laughed. "So a couple of points of business if I might." They both nodded their accord. "I understand that some folks from Washington want to talk to the dragon lady. Does that get you off the hook with Ed Pollito?"

"It should," the Sheriff said. "He also understands that Sonoma has first shot at her for the murder. Anyway, he has more than enough on his plate with the other three. They all lawyered up and then claimed they weren't properly Mirandized.

"You're kidding. Who did they get to represent them, Moe, Larry, and Curly?"

"Sort of. They were the high-priced spread, from the office that tried to get that Stanford swimmer off on appeal of that rape charge. Very expensive suits, and thinking they could steamroll over us country bumpkins. We record everything, and when it's a high profile or complicated case, we do it in front of someone from the DA's office, or a judge if one is available."

"So what happened?"

"The attorneys dropped the clients. The confessions were so detailed, they didn't have room to argue."

"Did they get new attorneys? So they might plead insanity based on monumental stupidity and greed?"

"Bloom's mother met with Ed – they went to school together – to find out what could be done. Ed told her they could offer to plead guilty and pay huge fines, and maybe get out early by going the good behavior route."

"Are they going to take his advice, Bogie?"

"I think so. She was told to find an attorney to handle the details pro forma."

Mike asked, "Any idea what kind of time they face?"

"Probably five or six years if they flip on the contractors which I presume they'll do. They were only involved in the money side of things. The attack on Douglass and the planned attack on Francie were instigated by the dragon lady."

A thought struck Francie. "Your people checked her over didn't they, I mean in her birthday suit?"

"Always do," the Sheriff responded.

"Any tattoos?"

"You thinking like the Tongs?"

Francie nodded.

"No nothing like that. I think I saw that she had a rose on her ankle."

The three were quiet as they thought about the disparity between the rose and the woman's actions. Mike broke the silence with a question.

"Francie, did you say something about finishing Wayne's book for him?"

"I was thinking about it, Mike, but that was when I thought a case would have to be made using the information he had put together to bring down these miscreants. But since they will be hoisted on their own petard, that won't be necessary. Besides, most people aren't interested in the details of property crimes. And anyone who cares will have gotten enough from the local coverage. Plus, Tony will write up the case, and he always produces a good read. That should be enough."

"What's happening with his Sea Ranch property?"

"I spoke with his son yesterday. A bright man, and honest like his father, as you'd expect. He asked me if I wanted to buy it, and for what his father paid for it – which would be a great deal – and without realtors. He has a family and they live in Brooklyn."

"A different world," Mike commented.

"Very different," Francie agreed. "I wasn't surprised that he wasn't interested in the house. But I was pleased that he had heard enough about me from his father to want to honor our relationship in this way."

"Very nice," said Bogie. "Are you going to going to take him up on it, France?"

She smiled. "I told him I would go up and pack all the personals and send them to him. And while I was up there, I'd think about his offer and the furnishings – Wayne did a quality job putting it all together – and get back to him. But I love my house in Mendocino, so I don't need it. But I don't know that I'm ready to let go of Wayne's house right away."

Mike and Bogie looked at each other, and then the sheriff, looking at their friend with a stern expression, said, "All right, you can say yes, but you can't move up there."

"No, absolutely not, Francie," Mike said with a commanding voice. "Weekends maybe, and the occasional vacation week, but you can't relocate. Crime here would go through the roof."

"I promise," Francie said, holding up her right hand. "So, you guys ready for some dessert?" She got up and walked to the kitchen.

"Dessert?" Bogie asked. "After that meal, I didn't think even Chez Francie would offer dessert."

She returned with the Jameson and three fresh glasses.

The Power Aphrodisiac

As you can imagine, a lot of people try to reach Francie LeVillard through me, her chronicler. At first I used to pay attention to their calls and emails, but it got to be too much. There was a flood of requests after the first volume of her stories was published, but few of them passed the smell – or sanity – test. Of those that seemed legitimate, at least on the surface, most were asking for investigations into cheating spouses, missing relatives, or contested inheritances, but none of these was the sort that would tickle Francie's detecting fancy even if they were legitimate.

When I showed her a sample of the requests that I was dismissing – some of them ardent pleas – Francie quickly agreed with my assessment. Her intuition was very strong and none, not even the close calls for me, got a second look from her. From then on, unless I felt there was real merit to a request, she didn't need to see them. So enfranchised, I got a new unlisted phone number and new email accounts.

I knew I risked putting up a barrier between Francie and

people who might be legitimate clients. But even though the world's finest consulting detective since Sherlock Holmes avoided the limelight, eschewing all press coverage – unless her visibility served a greater purpose – she never wanted for quality clients to engage her incredible skills. Yes, some people would try to enlist her services running into her at Trader Joe's or a restaurant or some public function, but Francie was quite capable of effectively dismissing those who refused to be politely brushed off.

I was more a public figure. I did some public speaking around the country, mostly at writers' conferences and to law enforcement groups. Happily, most of the participants understood that the registration fee did not entitle them to use me as a conduit to Francie and very few tried.

All that said, a number of times good friends or people coming through good friends, approached me to ask what they might do to deal with a situation that had confronted them. My friends were duly hesitant and they never pushed. That's what friends are about. On occasion people would think they were entitled to special access, but as I told them, those who thought they were entitled, by definition, weren't.

That said, a good number of Francie's cases came through people she or I knew, including top law enforcement, because they had a situation worthy of her attention. To be clear, that attention was not based on "thrill value" as in threats to life and limb, nor was it based on political purposes. And certainly not on the size of a promised fee. The case had to be interesting and noble.

It had to be of social value, as in righting a wrong or putting away dangerous criminals, and especially exposing people holding public office who had violated the public trust.

I should add that some of the most interesting cases have come through people we never would have thought might be involved or in touch with matters that were deserving of Francie's special skills. But in truth, many people living relatively quiet lives, or people important to them, have come upon information that will raise her professional eyebrows. And rarely have those eyebrows steered her wrong.

A case in point arose when I was breakfasting with dear Judith Anne (whose last name is kept private for obvious reasons). We had come to Hollister, about 45 miles from Carmel, to attend the wedding of her niece, and the next morning, before returning home, we had breakfast at J-J's.

I would be remiss if I didn't first provide a description of Hollister. It's where Judith Anne was born and raised, but unlike most of her friends, after she went away to college, she stayed away, living and working in Los Angeles, Chicago, and New York, before returning to California and the Monterey Peninsula.

Hollister is a sleepy sort of town. I recalled to her a television commercial that featured an older truck driver and a younger fellow going down the main street of a small city. The young man was awestruck. "I never believed Los Angeles was so big," he commented. "Son," said the older man, "This is Modesto."

Think *American Graffiti*, which was set in Modesto in 1962 (and released in 1973). Hollister was, and still is, smaller, but it is the county seat of San Benito County. Farming and ranching for the longest time, much of the land has been turned into middle- and higher-class housing. With a population of 38,000, it has mushroomed into a major bedroom community for people who are willing – or have no choice but – to bear the commute to the exploding San Jose megatropolis. Still, Hollister's main drag, San Benito Street, has retained much of its 1950s charm. Some buildings have been converted from prior uses, but for those who started life in Hollister as early baby-boomers, the ties to the past are real.

A long-time fixture in Hollister's downtown, Joella Jackson – yes, the owner of J-J's – was once a small-time Hollywood actress that you wouldn't remember, from films you never saw or even heard of. Maybe she had a dozen roles with a dozen lines of script in each. But she truly enjoyed making the films, and when her acting career was about to finish, she had no inkling she was about to make a life-changing move.

It happened that she was cast in what would be her final movie role as a cloistered nun – it was a silent part – in *Strawberry Road*. This independent, low-budget Japanese production was being shot in San Juan Bautista, which was known for where they shot the scary mission tower scene in *Vertigo* with James Stewart and Kim Novak.

When she wasn't needed on the set, Joella drove around, including through neighboring Hollister, and she fell in love with the area. So much so that she realized quite perspicaciously that she needed to change horses. So when all of her scenes had been shot, Joella hightailed it home, packed up her small if once-treasured life in Hollywood, and replanted herself in the more down to earth setting of Hollister. This was 1989 and the population was just under 19,000.

It was in her new hometown of Hollister, right there on the main drag, that she invested her new self in a new love, opening an eatery that catered to the locals' hunger for comfort food. *J-J's* menu featured familiar food that didn't require a dictionary. You know, a salad's a salad; people who wanted to play with arugula, jicama, frisbee, chicory, and escarole could go up the street to the fancy-schmancy restaurant in the hotel.

The locals soon became regulars, in part because the menu remained the same, there weren't a lot of specials, and what there were were no surprises. Plus, within six months Joella had recruited some of the best waitresses in town; they liked the way she treated her employees. What also attracted the serving talent was that J-J's served only breakfast and lunch (albeit seven days a week) which meant the workers were getting home before it got dark and had lives of their own. And maybe the biggest seller was the *Cheers*-like atmosphere "where everybody knows your name."

*   *   *   *   *

When Judith Anne and I had breakfast that Sunday morning in 2019, it was at an hour when most of the churches were pitching to hungry souls and J-J's was almost empty. Now being a veteran journalist as well as the chronicler of the Francie LeVillard mysteries, I had an interest in people who showed some mettle and struck out on their own, and soon Joella was sitting at our table telling us her story. Judith Anne had told me of Joella's Hollywood background in only the vaguest terms, because that's all there were, but the former denizen of the silver screen provided delicious and edifying bits and pieces that I knew would make a great book.

I told Joella if she would provide the details of her life in Tinseltown, I would produce a book for her. She confessed that she had thought about writing a book, and one that would interest not only the people who liked to read about the stars but also those who liked to learn what goes on behind the big screen.

She said she was definitely interested and that we should talk further about it. Then she peered at me and in a lower voice asked, "Are you a real journalist or one of those who's more interested in asking questions than getting answers?"

Judith Anne was taken aback that someone might ask such a question, but I smiled at her and then at Joella and said, "I not only want the answers, I want the truth." That put a look of satisfaction on her face.

"Then I've got a really big story for you. Not about me, but I've been trying to get attention to a situation that needs fixing – some corrupt people trying to get tax-payer money to fix something that's not broken."

Now when I was covering the news, both national and local on the East Coast, I heard scores of such tales, most of them raised by well-meaning people who either saw some real finagling or simply didn't understand how government and business collaborated, reasonably and legally. But there was something about the way Joella spoke to me that exiled most of my skepticism. Especially when she added a tag line.

"I think I've gotten myself into some trouble for asking too many questions."

I looked around casually, and realized that a nearby church must have gotten out because most of the tables were peopled, and that made it difficult where we were seated not to be overheard. "I understand what you are saying," I told her with steady eye contact, "but I think this conversation should take place in greater privacy."

Her eyes scanned the nearby diners and she slowly nodded her agreement. I took out a credit card and put it on the table, then pushed it toward her. She took the card and went behind the counter where she ran it and then brought it back to the table on the small plastic tray, putting it down in front of me. I filled in the tip, signed the tab, and handed it back to her, with my business card on the tray below the receipt. Quietly I told her, "Maybe you would call me from a business phone somewhere."

She gave me a broad customer "Thank-you" smile as she took the tray and went back behind the counter. Her call came that evening. She had a pre-paid phone, she told me, and was calling from the lobby of a hotel by the edge of town. She could see all around and no one was near enough to hear her.

"I hope you don't think I'm being paranoid, but when I

tell you what's happened already, I think you'll appreciate why I'm cautious." And then for the next ten minutes she told me what had happened over the past four months, once she had raised a hue and cry about some legally-questionable shenanigans taking place in the county, just outside of the Hollister city limits.

"No, I don't think you're paranoid, Joella. You're dealing with officials who have power and think they can bully common people into silence. You should keep your head down. I'm going to talk with Francie LeVillard about this. She has significant connections with law enforcement and she and they can figure out how to deal with what you've told me, without putting you at any risk."

There was a silence at the other end long enough to make me wonder if the call had been cut off. Just when I was about to speak, she replied with a deep sigh. Then, "I am so glad we met, Tony. I thought I was in the *Twilight Zone*, and I didn't know what to do."

"I'm sorry you had to get in as deep as you did, but your telling me about the situation will have important results. Just back off. I'll talk to Francie in the next day or so. She may want to talk to you in person, but that can be arranged so there is no further jeopardy for you."

"That's great. Thank you."

"One more thing, "I said, "if you would, make notes about everything that you told me, and anything else you might remember about these people, dates and times, relationships, et cetera. Even if it doesn't seem important, it may fit in with something that turns up later. Okay?"

"I'll do that. Should I email it to you or send it to the address on your card?"

"Either is fine. And you don't have to wait until you've scoured your memory. You can contact me as often as you want."

There was another deep sigh. "Thank you again. I feel so much better. My best to Judith Anne."

*   *   *   *   *

Before I called Francie, I wrote up my notes of the conversation with Joella Jackson. It didn't take long.

"I was thinking it might be you calling," Francie said when she picked up the phone.

"Funny how those things work."

"You have a case for me, I think."

"Okay, funny doesn't begin to describe it. Do you actually know something or are your intuitive powers working overtime?"

She chuckled. "Just a feeling, my friend."

"If you could only patent your process...."

"Yeah, but then I'd become famous and I'd have to hire security to fight off the groupies."

"And NSA would investigate you. Yeah, I know. Never mind. Just live your delicious quiet life here on the Central Coast."

She laughed. "Yup. So whatcha got?"

"What? Your intuition didn't supply the details?"

"It takes weekends off."

"Today's Thursday."

"Huh, well there's that." She laughed again. "So tell me."

And I did. I also emailed my notes to her, which included Joella's contact information. This is what I had written:

> Francie,
>
> Joella Jackson is a good, bright person. I say that because her Hollywood background could suggest a false stereotype. More to the point, she's a good citizen who has not only paid attention to how the local government is being run, but she has spoken up about it, and she is being bullied by some of the players.
>
> The city of Hollister appears to be in collusion with a major developer to provide public funds to aid in the delivery of water to yet another massive housing development on the south side of the city. The developers need larger pipes from the city's water supply to meet the needs of the incoming homeowners. Their argument in favor of the city covering the costs is a sizeable increase in the property tax base from the new residents.
>
> That doesn't sound unreasonable on the surface, but the developers have deep pockets and could easily afford to pay for the new pipes themselves, what with the large profits

they expect to make selling the new houses. They already have contracts on more than half of the properties, and they have yet to pour a single foundation.

Another issue is that three of the five city council members have invested in the development. So has the county administrator. And some of their friends and families have been offered special deals to buy property there.

Now this is hardly a surprise. It must happen everywhere there is a need for housing. But here is where it gets particularly ugly. Last winter, during the heavy rains, there was an emergency discharge from a water treatment facility that sits on a hill above the development site. The water caused a minor mudslide that tore up Southside Road, an important two-lane route half-way down the hill.

The city and county officials argued for a while over who should have to fix the road, and what needed to be done. The main question was do they patch it or make major repairs. Now you, being a former journalist, must already be smelling the underside of this issue. The major repairs would not only be expensive, but would also involve replacing the existing water pipes that weren't damaged but run under the old road with new ones. Surprise, surprise.

There is another complication in this story. It

has to do with the emergency water release. First, there's a question about whether there needed to be that propitious opening of the emergency discharge pipeline. The water in the holding pond wasn't near the level that it needed to be lowered.

But worse, an old homeless fellow named Tom Finn was known to camp out in the five-foot emergency discharge pipe, and he was in it the night the water was released. He was shot out of the pipe by the force of the water and fell twenty feet onto the rocks below and was killed. No one knew he was there that night, and no one is suggesting that this was anything but an accident, but when Joella asked at a hearing on Old Tom's death why the water was released that night, she was told it was normal procedure; that the water department officials had no reason to think the man was in the pipe that night.

Joella doesn't think he was deliberately murdered, but she thinks the emergency release was no emergency. She thinks they just screwed up. Fatally, as it were, and they won't admit it. Yes, my friend, like Watergate and how many other governmental scandals, the cover up is worse than the original mistake.

In addition to raising the issue at the hearing, she wrote a letter to the editor of the *Hollister Record*, the local newspaper, saying she didn't get satisfactory answers from the local officials about the emergency water release. And that's when she started getting harassed. There were a couple of letters to the editor complaining that Joella was just trying to cause trouble because she didn't want Hollister to change, that she was a hippie tree-hugger. The names on the letters were untraceable.

Then things got worse. A couple or three or four people would come into her restaurant and find fault with the food, sending things back, refusing to pay. She recognized a couple of these people as city staffers who worked for the council members who were invested in the development. Not to be cowed by such behavior, she arranged to have one or another good friend in her restaurant at all hours. If such a scene were created, the person would tape the rudeness and then confront the offenders, promising to upload the video to FB, etc. if they ever treated Joella like that again. That seemed to have done the trick. Only one other table pulled that nonsense again, so word must have gotten out. It got out even more effectively when the video of the rudeness was posted on several social media platforms.

The latest harassment was that when Joella has been driving home from the restaurant, she has been followed by the same county deputy several times who has stopped her telling her first that a taillight was out. Another time he gave her a ticket for driving three miles over the speed limit. And a third time, he claimed that she was driving erratically and gave her an alcohol breath test. Well, the taillight wasn't out, she made it a point to always drive under the speed limit, and she's been a teetotaler since she left Hollywood many years ago.

Francie, I know how this kind of thing burns you, as it does me. Especially citizens being treated this way by politicians using cops to shut them up. I wonder if I might set up a meeting for her with you.

Best, Tony

*   *   *   *   *

Francie was right on it. She called me not long after I had emailed her Joella's story. "These people need to be seriously punished, Tony. How do we proceed?"

"Good, Francie. I knew this would raise your hackles. I suggest you meet with Joella...not in Hollister, it's a very gossipy place, and you might be recognized. I was thinking that I could fly her back to Monterey and you two could meet at the Fly Away Café for an hour."

"Smart." There was a brief silence, and then she said, "And why don't you fly over the area in question. Do a couple of obvious circles."

It was my turn to be silent as I considered the implications of her suggestion. "As in, someone could correlate the tail number of the plane with me, and finding out that I'm a journalist, that could make some waves."

"Or at least start them talking, yes. I don't think they would get violent, but knowing that Joella is connected to a real pro, outside of the Hollister community, could provide an added layer of protection."

"Right."

"But, Tony, give me a couple of days before you contact her about 'flying over the crime scene' as it were. I have a couple of calls to make."

"Thanks, Francie. And, yes, I'll wait for your call."

*   *   *   *   *

One of her calls resulted in Francie meeting with Mike Olsen, the FBI's regional director, whose office was in Salinas. He and Francie had worked together on a number of cases, ranging from fraud to dealing with assassins from the Russian mob. Francie had also worked closely with the Monterey County Sheriff, Telford "Bogie" Spivac, and on some matters, all three worked together. She thought to bring in the sheriff but wanted to run the case by the FBI man to see if his federal position might be needed.

They met for lunch at the clubhouse at Corral de Tierra where Mike had a membership, mostly for business though he did get out on the links from time to time. They found a table in a corner of the deck overlooking the fairways, and away from the few other diners. They looked over the menu and ordered quickly. Then Francie told Mike what she had learned from me and then on her own, and what she wanted to do about it.

When she had finished, she asked Mike if he agreed that the sheriff should be brought in, or at least, briefed. "Yes, he should know everything you told me. What with all the mess just over the county line, he may have picked up some loose ends that could help to tie your case together."

"That was my thought. I'll ring him this afternoon."

"Good, and I'll take care of what you need."

*　　*　　*　　*　　*

Francie's call from her car found the sheriff leaving his office for a meeting in Monterey. He would be finished by four-thirty and could meet Francie at five. He suggested the bar-restaurant at the top of the Monterey Tides. They arrived at the elevator together a couple of minutes before five, and soon were seated with a broad view of Monterey Bay in front of them and drinking down a couple of Happy Hour Sierra Nevadas.

"I'm glad you brought me in on this, Francie," he said after he learned the lay of the Hollister political land. "There was always something too slick about the current batch of pretend cowboys."

"Do you know more about the players that I should know?"

The sheriff sighed. "First the pols over there aren't very bright. They're mostly retailers who applied their egos and sales pitch skills to getting elected to the council. They like getting a good table at the Olive Garden."

Francie chuckled. "I know that type all too well from my years in television news."

"I don't doubt it. The developers are actually local, but recently they made a lot of money putting up a lot of bricks and mortar in the middle years of the Silicon Valley boom, and moved to Hollister to live in their scaled-down McMansions, and plan their next foray into converting farm and grazing lands into middle to upscale developments."

"Are they crooks?"

"No, not really, but they're only out for the money. They push, they wheedle, to get permits, water rights, new roads, et cetera, but they keep it legal."

"That's what I found, too. No rap sheets, but more than their share of doling out and receiving big favors and special treatment." She signaled the waiter for two more bottles. "Any idea who would be trying to bully Joella Jackson?"

"Yeah," he began, and when he saw the waiter approaching with their new drinks, he held his tongue. The ales were put on the table and the empties removed. When the waiter left, Bogie handed Francie a bottle, took the other for himself, and they gently clinked them.

"I think I've only seen the county administrator once or twice at multi-county hearings. It's just hearsay, but it's said that he thinks highly of himself, although I've also heard that he knows his limitations. He's got a cushy job and has no plans to go anywhere – Sacramento or Washington – because he loves living here. If anyone should know what's going on, it would be the top dog, Herbert Colossino."

The sheriff laughed. "A funny thing, he actually likes to

be called Herbert. He's made that clear to more than one councilman who called him Herb. One called him Herbie and the look on Colossino's face was ice. He doesn't suffer fools, gladly or otherwise. But he knows the difference between stupid and corrupt."

Francie was quiet. "Sounds like a man who would flex his bureaucratic muscle if need be, but it would never lead to violence."

Bogie nodded. "That's right. I think maybe he puts a forceful image forward, but I have to tell you that I have heard from people I respect that the bottom line is that he's better than his image."

"Bogie, did you get any inside dope on the emergency water discharge, the one where the homeless man was in the pipe and got killed?"

"You heard about that?" She nodded. He went on, "Of course you would. Well, I don't think it was anything but an accident. Not deliberate. I don't think they knew he was in the pipe that night, but they knew he was sometimes. You'd think someone would hike down a little ways to the mouth of the pipe and shine a light in."

"But they didn't."

"No. The number two of the county water board said, from what he knew, the guy had been seen in town less than an hour earlier. They must have presumed he was safely out of harm's way, if they even thought about him."

"That's at least gross malfeasance if not involuntary manslaughter."

"Francie, if every incompetent or perpetrator of malfea-sance was punished, there would be no one left in the civil service. As regards the manslaughter charge, all of these people in government in a place like Hollister have known each other for years, often decades. They went to school together. Their kids go to school together. They protect each other to the extent that they can."

*   *   *   *   *

The next day, Francie awoke to find an email sent early that morning from Mike Olsen concerning her sugges-tion that a U.S. attorney in San Jose file orders for wiretaps on the phones of the three city council mem-bers under suspicion, Herbert Colossino, the county administrator, four of the principal developers, Molly Swinglet, the water board official, and a name she had added the day before, Ben Suharto, the supervisor of the water treatment plant.

She called me to say that she was ready to meet with Joella Jackson, and the next two days were free, if I was and the whistleblower could be. I was and checked to see if one of my favorite planes to rent would be avail-able during the middle of the day for three hours. As it happened, the weather forecasters had messed up again – all their forecasting models had been rendered close to useless by climate change – and had said it would be low fog most of the day. So no one reserved an aircraft. But the sun was out and I took advantage of it. I checked with Joella who said she was ready, able, and excited to see the crime scene from above. That's the way I had put it to her, but she knew it meant more than flying a couple of circles over the water treatment operation. I told her I would pick her up in front of the old Ding-a-Ling restaurant at the Hollister Airport. I got the name from an aviation site that hadn't tracked the gastronomic changes.

"That goes back a ways," she said. "It was closed for a while, moved into town, and the city fixed up the airport buildings and now Seabrisa's Eatery is there. Not that we're going to be eating there. Just so you know if you're looking for signs."

"Thanks, Joella. I'll park on the ramp in front. Be there at eleven if that's good for you."

"That's good for me. See you then."

Indeed, as I was touching down, I saw her standing in front of the recently-painted building that housed the new airport restaurant. I taxied back from the far end of the airport, and three minutes later she was all strapped into the co-pilot's seat with a headset on, and we were communicating on the intercom. I restarted the aircraft and taxied back to the runway. Soon we were in the air again, headed for the south side of Hollister. I made two wide circles above the water treatment plant, noting the slide area below the emergency discharge pipe which had been cleaned up when the road had been repaired, after the large new pipes had been installed. Even from three thousand feet, the new housing development look huge. Because it was. Finally I broke away and flew us to Monterey.

I was pleased to see that Francie had come to the AeroDynamic Aviation field operation rather than wait for us at the Fly Away Café. I parked the aircraft and shut it down. I let Joella out of her side and brought her over to meet Francie who was walking toward us.

"Why don't you ladies go over to the restaurant while I see to the plane. I'll be over in about ten minutes."

Francie smiled appreciatively, and they walked off toward the terminal building and the restaurant. I signaled Annie through the office window and she pressed the button that opened the security gate for them. Even though I would be flying Joella back to Hollister in an hour, I tied down the plane and asked Annie to make sure it was refueled. I was not in a hurry to get to lunch. I thought it would be good for Francie and Joella to get to know each other, which would be easier without my being there.

I made my unhurried way to the Fly Away Café, and seeing the two women in a booth by the window, I steered over to the bar. After a few minutes, Francie looked over at the entrance, and in a wider look found me. She smiled, shook her head, and nodded. I smiled back. Francie said something. Joella looked surprised as she cast a glance in my direction. Francie explained what I was doing, and Joella shot me a broad smile.

I ordered a sandwich and ate at the bar. Looking over at them to make sure they didn't need me – they didn't – but when she had found out what she needed to know and given Joella her instructions, Francie gave me a quick signal to join them. As I did, they got up from the booth. It was time to get Joella back to Hollister. We walked back to AeroD together, and Francie, a pilot herself, helped Joella into the aircraft and to get strapped in.

"I don't think you're in any danger, Joella, but you might keep your eyes open. If you get into trouble, don't hesitate to call 9-1-1. But again, these people aren't violent. Maybe to the environment but not to people."

"I know you're right, Francie. And thank you for all your time and effort. These folks are gonna regret ever messing with us."

They laughed together. Francie pushed the door shut, and I reached across Joella to lock it. Thirty minutes later, I was leaning across an empty seat to secure the door again. The game was a-foot.

*　　*　　*　　*　　*

Two days later, Francie checked in with Mike Olsen to find out if the wiretaps were in place.

"Yes, and they've been fruitful. Oh, no one admitted anything, or talk about their dirty deeds. But there was plenty of collaboration in their chats. It wasn't the typical patter you'd expect of business associates. Too personal."

"That fits."

"Yep. Juries love this sort of evidence. Oh, it's not evidence, but they know what it means."

She told Mike that she was going to Hollister and would be gone for a few hours. If he didn't hear from her by late afternoon, he might ask after her. She didn't imagine she'd be in any danger, but maybe someone wanted to ask her questions.

"Francie..."

"Mike, not to worry. I'm leaving a very visible trail." He growled. "Tell you what, I'll meet you at Café Fina at six. You can see for yourself. And I should have some quality dope for you."

"Okay, sure. You're smarter and more clever than any of the crooks I know. But yes, I'll take you up on the dinner invitation. I have an appointment over there at five. You're giving me an excuse to leave early if I feel like it."

"Which you will."

"Which I will." When she ended the call, she made another, to the restaurant. Roxanne answered the phone and wrote down the reservation.

"Is this business or pleasure?"

"Both, Mike Olsen."

"He's good guy. Do you still want table nine?"

"Roxy, I always want table nine, unless downstairs is noisy, then —."

"I know, twenty-two."

Francie laughed. "See you at six. Thanks."

*   *   *   *   *

Francie probably looked too fashionable to be lunching at a place like J-J's, but she wanted to be noticed if the wrong people were watching the place. She went through a salad and iced tea at a leisurely pace, and when she was done, she eschewed dessert. Joella brought her the check. Francie covered it with cash and went back to the ladies' room. If anyone was seriously tracking events, they would have seen Joella go back into the kitchen. At one point she came out to say a few words to her waitress who was standing in front of the pastry counter. Then she disappeared into the kitchen again.

Less than a minute later, anyone watching from the front of the restaurant would have seen the woman ducking out by the back door, getting into her car, and driving away. She turned south on San Benito, then east on Nash for a half-dozen blocks before turning south again on Airline Highway, Joella's regular route home. It was not far past Union Road that the deputy's car started looming larger in the rearview mirror. She had seen where he had been parked by the restaurant and made sure he wouldn't lose her.

A few miles on, the deputy turned on his flashing lights, and when he was fifty yards behind her, he added the siren. She carefully slowed the car and pulled over on the side of the road in a safe spot. Then she waited as the deputy radio'd in, then got out of his car looking over hers, until he got to her door. Her window was closed. He knocked on it. Keeping her eyes straight ahead, she touched the switch to open the window.

"You know what you were doing this time?"

"I was driving down Airline Highway to go visit a friend."

Her voice caught him up short. He bent over and looked in the car window. That's when the driver turned her head and looked directly at him.

He stepped back abruptly. "Hey, you're not... Hey, what's going on here? Who are you?"

"Were you expecting someone else, officer?"

"Where's Joella? What are you doing driving her car?"

"I believe Joella is at her restaurant, officer. Where she's been most of the day. As far as driving her car, why, I was driving it very safely, driving under the speed limit, and observing all traffic laws."

A deep scowl was a clue that he was out of his element, and in over his head. "How come you look like her?"

"Oh, officer, do you think so? What a lovely compliment."

That didn't satisfy him. He tried "What's going on here?" again.

"You asked that already, officer. Is there anything else, or may I go?"

"No, you can't."

"Why not? I haven't broken any laws. You haven't even asked for my driving license and the registration."

"Yeah, I want to see those."

"But officer, you have given me no reason why I should. You haven't said why you have stopped me, and until you do, I'm within my rights to withhold the documents."

"What, are you, a lawyer or something?"

"Deputy..." she read the name tag above his badge..."Freylinghausn. I'm you're worst nightmare."

*   *   *   *   *

Three hours later, Mike Olsen was laughing so hard that

tears came to his eyes. "You didn't say that?" he insisted.

Francie laughed. "No, but I thought it, and gave him a big smile." They were sitting at the downstairs table, enjoying a special Italian red from Dominic's private cellar, and nibbling on some new hors d'oeuvres he was taste-testing on his friends. "I told him if he didn't have any more business with me, then I'd be on my way. Otherwise, I wanted to call my attorney and have him meet us at the sheriff's office."

"Good girl," the FBI man said with enthusiasm. "And that was enough."

"Actually, it took him a moment to realize that I was letting him off, though not in those terms."

"More like he was getting away with something."

"That was my take." She shook her head. "Anyway, he took a step back, looked at me again, and then went back to his car. Then he got in and drove away."

"You had set all this up when Tony flew her over to Monterey?"

"Yes. It wasn't very complicated. She and I are roughly the same size, and of course she had an extra uniform and a wig. It didn't have to fit perfectly since I was mostly to be observed from a distance. I went to the ladies' room and got dressed. Joella came in and gave me the keys to her car. And yes, she had checked to make sure the registration was in the glove box."

Mike shook his head with pride.

"What did you get from the taps?" Francie asked. "Did he call anyone?"

"Yes, as a matter of fact. He called Colossino's office. Asked for the boss but was sidetracked by his chief aide. It was very interesting. It sounded like she was worried about being overheard. She tried to get Freylinghausn to shut up, but the deputy didn't get it. He talked about trying to stop Joella, and wound up stopping a stranger who looked like her in her car."

"Why would she worry about a tap do you think?"

"I know they didn't find anything since our wires are in the telco offices."

"And nobody there shares information?"

He shook his head slowly. "Not when it's the feds. They know they'd get in too much trouble. Not only prison time, but they'd lose their pension."

"That gives you some leverage."

"That's what most of the old-timers who handle the back room are staying on the job for."

Roxanne arrived with their main course. Both were having Dungeness crab, Francie's cold in an Asian vinaigrette, and Mike's hot in Dominic's amazing cioppino sauce. Both would clean their plates.

*　　*　　*　　*　　*

At seven the next morning, the FBI man was in his car not a block from Freylinghausn's house. The deputy had bought it when he was married, with help from his parents, and the value had appreciated dramatically over their thirty years in it. It's going to be a miracle if he doesn't lose it, Mike thought, as he sipped at his coffee. The deputy should be leaving his house in five minutes;

he was very regular.

When he saw the front door open, Mike got out of his car and started down the sidewalk. The deputy's car was always parked on the street, in the event of an emergency. Little did he know. The two men arrived at his car about the same time.

"I'm Mike Olsen, FBI." He held his ID in front of him but not so anyone watching them might notice. "I need to talk to you at my office in Salinas."

"What this about?"

"Oh, I think you know. Harassing Joella Jackson, for starters." He held up his hand when the deputy started to protest. He looked hard into the man's face. "It's over," he declared firmly. "But you're the first one we're talking to, and you know what that means. You could do yourself some good if you cooperate."

Francie arrived in Mike's outer office at eight. As they had planned, the deputy was waiting alone in the conference room. She was wearing the waitress outfit and the wig because she knew Mike would get a kick out of it, and Freylinghausn wouldn't.

"You look like the Candy Clark character in *American Graffiti*," Mike said.

"She was a favorite of Joella Jackson's. That's why she wears the wig."

"Well, it certainly is different, but," he shook his head, smiling, "it's also certainly not you."

"Oh dang. And I was thinking I needed a new look."

He chuckled, and added in an affectionate tone, "You always look good, Francie."

"Thank you, Mike." She nodded to the conference room door. "How's our perp doing?"

"He been rocked. I gave him an outline of what he was facing, but I don't think it's gotten through to him."

"Hmm, I thought he might need the blunt instrument approach when he stopped me yesterday. Not the sharpest knife in the proverbial drawer."

"No, not nearly." He opened the door and let Francie walk in first. The deputy's face showed shock.

"Hey, what is she doing here?"

Mike and Francie took seats at each end of the table. When the two of them were questioning him, the deputy would be switching his attention left and right.

Mike answered his question. "She's going to explain to you just how much trouble you're in over your would-be traffic stop."

The deputy didn't understand but turned his attention to Francie.

She took off the wig and put it on an empty chair. Her own hair was dark and coiffed short; as she put it, to make sure her hair never got in her eyes when she was using a gun. "I put a device in the car called Precision GPS. It registers location with a dual axis of less than six inches. And it measures velocity to within a half-mile per hour. It also taps into the car's maintenance control device and registers all factors of the engine operation from oil temperature to fuel consumption, battery, lights function, et cetera, electronically. And it transmits all the data live via satellite to a website.

The deputy winced. It was more out of confusion than awareness of his worsening situation.

"What it means for you, Deputy Freylinghausn, is that it produced an unassailable record that from the time I pulled away from the restaurant, my car never exceeded the speed limit by even a half-mile per hour, never crossed the centerline, took every turn smoothly, and never once violated traffic laws or safety standards."

Mike waited a short while for the deputy to process what he heard and then helped him along. "What that means is that there is scientific proof that you had no cause, even marginal, to pull over her car."

"But," he protested, "I didn't know it wasn't her, I mean, that it was her."

Francie managed to keep a straight face as her eyes flicked over at Mike. He looked back at her and she picked up the interrogation. "What you're saying is that you thought it was Joella Jackson? That you were pulling her over to cite her, even though she hadn't done anything wrong?"

"Um, well I wasn't sure. I thought she had done something."

"What did you think she had done?"

"I don't know," his confusion and the frustration came out. "I don't remember. I was just doing my job."

"Ahso," Mike said encouragingly. "And who told you that was your job, to pull over Ms. Jackson. As you had three other times in the past month, for a taillight that wasn't out, for driving over the speed limit which she never does, and to give her an alcohol breath test when she doesn't drink. And then you pulled over someone you thought was Ms. Jackson, and all of that case is recorded."

"Strike four," said Francie coolly.

The deputy sat slouched in his chair, looking down at his hands in his lap, not looking up, not saying a word.

Mike leaned forward slightly, his forearms on the table. "Wake up, Freylinghausn. This isn't about getting a rap on the knuckles. Unless you unload, and I mean all of it and right now, you're going to prison. Judges don't like crooked cops. And if you think your connections are going to get you out of trouble, you don't get that you are not going up before some local judge who's friends with your friends. This is a federal case."

Francie looked up at Mike, got his attention, and with a slight nod, signaled that they should go out of the room. When they did, she asked him, "He's just dumb, isn't he?"

"That's my take."

"What about telling him you recorded him calling Colossino and talking to his aide?"

He nodded thoughtfully, "Yes, and I have a good angle on it."

They walked back inside and after closing the door behind them, just stood there, looking down at the deputy. "Listen, we've got recordings of you calling one of your pals." That caused him to finally look up at them. "That's right. Yesterday, when you called Colossino but he didn't want to talk to you. You talked to Megan Riels, and she kept trying to shut you up, but you didn't get it, did you? I think she was worried about there being a tap on their phone."

What color was left in Freylinghausn's face seemed to drain before their eyes. Mike told him how precarious was his position. "Come on. You know how it works. Whoever spills the beans first is going to be dealt a better hand. And the more beans, the better chance of a Get out of Jail Free card. You know, depending how much you tell us and how fast. Do you think Megan Riels is going to hold out? We go in with that recording, and it's gonna be songbird time, and she'll be singing your way behind bars."

They sat in silence for over a minute, and then Francie and Mike got up to leave.

Mike told him, "We only have a holding cell for you here, Freylinghausn. We're going to have to send you up to the federal facility in San Jose. That's where you'll be formally arrested and get your phone call." He opened the door and called for an agent to put the deputy in the holding cell.

"One more thing, deputy," Francie said before he was led away. "If you think of fighting this instead of cooperating, you're going to wind up with a lawyer who will spend a lot of your money."

"You'll probably lose your house as well as your pension," Mike put in.

"And you'll be facing people in the jury box, most of whom have been stopped for traffic offenses, and they'll see you as a good way to get back at the system." She shook her head. "I'm not telling you something you don't know. I just don't understand why you won't help yourself. These people you think of as your friends, they have been using you. But they aren't violent. They wouldn't hurt you, but they'd sell you out in a Hollister minute. They would like you to fall on their sword."

"Think about it, Freylinghausn. I'll be sending you up to San Jose at noon." He looked at his watch. "You've two hours to come to your senses." With that he nodded to the agent who took over.

"You know the drill," the agent said. "Turn around and hands behind your back." Freylinghausn did so, and as Francie and Mike walked away they heard the sound of the handcuffs clicking down on his wrists.

* * * * *

Francie saved herself another trip to Hollister by phoning Molly Swinglet at her water department office. Saying she was writing an article about real Californians with their hand on the spigot during the drought and now a good year for water, Francie easily got her to take her call. After buttering her up with several questions about how she managed such an important job, Francie turned to the kinds of challenges that people in her position had to deal with that the public would rarely hear about, and would appreciate her efforts.

"So, the night Tom Finn was killed, what happened?" she asked.

The was a silence that chilled more every second.

Francie cut into it. "I understand from reading in the *Hollister Record* that you had been with friends that night, when you were driving by the water treatment plant on your way home, you saw a light on in the control room, and you went up there to check it out." She paused. "That was very brave of you, a woman, going up there alone in the middle of the night."

Francie could hear the confusion in the woman's silence. "They said you went up there and found the emergency discharge operating, but no one there. Is that right?"

Slowly came a "yes".

"Well, it was lucky you knew how it worked so you could turn it off." Francie chuckled audibly. "I mean, I don't think there are a lot of executives who would know how to turn it off. Good for you."

"Uh, thanks."

"And so, when you were there, Ben Suharto, showed up, and he made sure everything was as it was supposed to." No response. "And he came by because there was a silent alarm that notified him because no one was on duty but he was on call at home."

"We can't afford to staff the place 24/7/365."

"No, of course not." More silence and then Francie asked, "So it was apparent that someone had broken into the operations room and opened the emergency discharge pipe and then left." No comment. "A glass panel in the door had been smashed to get in."

"Yeah. There was glass on the floor inside."

Robotic response, thought Francie. "But so why would anyone do that? I mean, what was there to gain? Who would want to block Southside Road? Who benefitted?"

"I don't know. The police didn't find out."

"Not yet," Francie corrected. "There was a report that some of the people up at the water treatment plant knew about Old Tom sleeping in the discharge tunnel some nights."

"Uh, I guess. I don't know."

"But who would have wanted to kill him?"

"No one," she replied anxiously. "No one would have. It must have been a mistake. Whoever did it didn't know he slept there, or didn't think he was there that night."

"And so they didn't think to check?"

"No. They wouldn't."

"Well, Ms. Swinglet," Francie said in a satisfied voice, "you've been a great help. I really appreciate all that you've told me."

"But...oh, sure. You're welcome."

Francie sighed deeply after she hung up the phone. As much as she didn't like cheats, especially those in government, she knew that people like Swinglet weren't the brains behind the crimes. They were complicit victims, and they would suffer exponentially more for their misdeeds.

She called Mike Olsen and told him of her conversation.

"Good. It's what you thought."

"Do you have Suharto?"

"He said he'd be here in twenty minutes.

"Do you need anything? Donuts?"

"Fer crying out loud, Francie, I'm not a cop."

She laughed, "I'll be there in thirty."

"Don't speed, my friend. You'll only get yourself in trouble."

When she arrived, it was with donuts and coffees, and she was in an ostentatiously chipper mood. She chattered about how well the investigation was going and shook her head when she talked about how all politicians lied the same, whether they worked on Capitol Hill or in Hollister. Then she smiled directly at Suharto who had been rubbing his hands together nervously in his lap. "Do you take cream?" she wanted to know.

It did take him a moment to catch up with her, but he managed to shake his head and then say "yes". She pushed a cup of coffee across the table to him, and a napkin, spoon, and container of creamer. Again in a declarative voice she informed him, "I brought sugar, too, if you want any." He shook his head and stuck with that answer. "Please enjoy a donut," she continued as she opened a box of mixed donuts. "I got them at Red's in Monterey. I'm not sure they aren't the best in the county." She handed him a small paper plate, and insistently waited for him to choose one. "Yes, those maple ones are some of my favorites. Maybe because I was brought up in the northeast."

Later Francie told Mike how much she would have liked

to look over at him to see his response to her show, but she knew he would maintain a poker face.

"He was totally lost," he told her. "I thought he might need a change of drawers."

It got worse for him when Francie took a coffee, black, and sat down across from Suharto. Then in an even voice she told him, "You won't believe why I'm in such a good mood."

He looked at her, not sure if she was expecting an answer from him. She went on. "Because I just got off a call with Molly Swinglet, and she told me the wildest story about what happened that night Tom Finn was killed." She let that sink in. "I say killed rather than murdered because I'm sure his killing wasn't deliberate. I think it was just a mistake. Negligence...involuntary manslaughter. Of course it's still serious. A felony, punishable by two to four years in prison and a fine up to $10,000. And if you," she emphasized the pronoun, "are convicted of being an accessory after the fact, why you're still facing sixteen months to three years, and a $5,000 fine."

She looked directly at the man, all hint of a smile gone. "You haven't touched your donut," she observed.

Suharto took a deep breath and let it out. He looked up at Francie and asked in a lifeless voice, "What do you want to know?"

"All of it," she replied coldly. "And don't leave anything out."

He nodded. He looked down at the table in front of him. And suddenly, he reached out for the donut, and in a couple of bites it was gone. He sighed, "I'm the supervisor of the water treatment plant, and because they keep cutting our budget, I'm the one who is called if there is a problem, day and night, forty-nine weeks a year, just excepting my vacation time. And if there's no one there to call if something goes wrong, if anyone enters the plant, or if there is a major change in the equipment settings, then I'm alerted on my cellphone. But the plant is a simple operation, so I'm never called.

"But that night, my phone alarm went off, first with entry into the building and then with a notice that the emergency discharge valve had been opened. This was ten-thirty-seven at night. No one should have been there, and the valve should not have been opened, especially full. You never do that. Almost always we open it maybe ten percent. So I was already in bed – I get up early – and I threw on some clothes and drove to the plant. I was there at ten-fifty-three."

Francie gave a slight nod of appreciation at his professional eye on the time.

"When I got there, I recognized Molly's car out front. I went in and she was surprised to see me."

"Excuse me," Francie asked, "but wasn't she aware of the alarm system?"

"Apparently not."

"Go on."

"I asked what she was doing there. I knew right away that she was trying to make up a story, but I was already going to the board to close the emergency discharge valve. She didn't say anything as I shut it off. Then I turned around and just looked at her. We didn't really know each other. I think she'd been out to the plant for a couple of board meetings, but there'd been no need to talk to each other. She sure knew who I was.

"Then it was like really weird. It was as though she hadn't broken in and everything was all right, that she hadn't opened the valve." He shook his head. "She said, 'So Ben, we're really pleased with the job you've been doing, and there's talk that maybe you should be on the water board. You could keep your job, of course, but being on the board has a decent stipend and a number of perks, including a county car.'

"I nodded my head slowly as I was waiting for the punch line. It took maybe a whole minute, and then she said, 'So here's what happened. I was driving by on Southside Road and I saw a light on here in the office. I couldn't imagine what was happening, so I drove up to find out. And I saw the door was open, and the window in the door was broken and so I went in. I saw that the emergency discharge, uh, dial was on, and so I turned it off.'

"I think I looked at her like she was partly off the rails. Then she went on. "And then you drove up, and made sure everything was the way it should be, that the dial was off. And I showed you the glass on the floor where someone had broken in from the outside.' Then she nodded at me a couple of times and walked out of the office. I stood watching her through the open door as she got into her car and drove away."

"Did she ever follow up with you about what happened?"

He shook his head.

"Have you heard anything about an appointment to the water board?"

"Yeah, a couple of days later I got a memo from Ms. Riels in the county administrator's office saying I was being considered for an appointment to the water board, and would I send her an updated résumé."

"And did you?"

"Yeah."

Francie looked hard at him. "What were you thinking?"

He didn't answer immediately. "I guess I wasn't. My explanation to myself was that the story she gave the paper was, well, plausible, I guess. And I knew I'd be in all sorts of trouble if I came out with a different story."

"And if you didn't rock the boat, you'd get the seat on the water board."

"Actually, that wasn't a big deal for me. They don't do much, and what they do usually messes things up. But what I was really concerned about was losing my job. I work at the pleasure of the country." He shrugged. "So I went along with it. The investigators asked me what happened. No, they told me what Ms. Swinglet had said and asked if I had anything to add. I knew the fix was in so I said I didn't. When the paper called, I told them to ask her, and they didn't ask me again."

"Did you know why she did this?"

"I didn't know, but I figured it had something to do with the new development going in up the road. Opening the valve caused the ground to shift and broke up Southside Road a good bit. When they repaired it, they put in larger pipes which gave the developers more water and they could build more houses." He shrugged. "Isn't it always about somebody getting rich?"

Mike put in, "It's not always about someone getting killed."

Suharto shook his head. "Yeah, no, I know. I mean, you're right. She didn't know about Old Tom sleeping in the discharge pipe. It was a total accident. But we didn't find out about it for a couple of weeks. His body had washed across the road and down the slope. Then it had been covered with mud and other debris. And by then, her story had been accepted, you know. Why not?"

Francie noted, "And you had backed her up."

"Yeah. I'm not making excuses. I'm just telling you how it happened." He reached back and rubbed his neck hard. "For what it's worth, I haven't slept well since they found Old Tom. He and I went to school together. We used to go fishing together. I saw him around town. One of my people told him to stay out of the pipe because of the emergency discharges we did every three months, and he said he would. I don't think he believed him. But we only did a ten percent flow, which wasn't a big deal. He would have heard it coming and had plenty of time to get out before the water reached him. He wouldn't have gotten shot out of there like what must have happened." Pain was etched in his face. He shook his head. "I'm really sorry about him." He took another deep breath and let it out. "But when we found out about him, well, there was nothing I could do."

Francie couldn't hide her empathy but still managed to keep a cold edge in her voice. "You could have told what happened. You could have told the truth."

He nodded his head. "Now I have."

"One more thing, Mr. Suharto," Francie said, "to be clear. You can't go back on what you told us. If Swinglet doesn't plead, though I expect she will, and her case goes to court, you will have to testify. And the prosecutor will ask you under oath, 'Did you believe the story Ms. Swinglet told you?' There will be no room for equivocation."

He shook his head. "Not anymore."

Mike pushed a legal pad and a couple of pens over to Suharto. "I want you to think back about anything else you might remember now. Who, what, when, where... anything to add to what you've told us. We'll leave you alone for fifteen minutes."

"Okay." He pulled the pad and pens across to himself. Then he looked over from Mike to Francie. "I have told you the truth. I'll try to remember some more details. But I need to tell you, I'm kind of relieved that you called me in."

Francie nodded her recognition of what he said. Then she and Mike left him alone, sitting down in the lobby where they could talk and keep an eye on the conference room door. Not that they were worried about his trying to leave. It's what you do.

"You had his phone?" Francie asked.

"Yes. He handed it over when he arrived. He knew what

was coming."

"Any calls?"

"No, actually. But our tap picked up a call from Swinglet to Riels. She asked for Colossino but he was 'unavailable'... even though she said it was important."

Francie thought a moment. "I wonder if we should give them credit for sensing the walls were coming down."

"I'd like to think it was that, rather than our efforts were somehow being leaked."

Francie shook her head. "Really? I don't think so. There are so few ties between the feds and the locals. Not impossible, but not likely. I hope. What did you think of him?"

"I guess I'm not surprised at what he told us."

"And how he got into this mess? That was my feeling. So easy to fall down the rabbit hole. When you're worried about your situation. When the people calling the shots control your future and they're crooks."

"And they don't care a whit about you, except what it takes to buy you off."

"Yes. I don't think they had any idea about who he was. Nor did they care."

"Do you think they could mess up the investigation by telling people what we asked them and what was said?"

"They could but I told them that anything that we talked about or they told us had to remain completely confidential. Couldn't be shared with anyone, not even family. If we ever found out that they did, we would charge them with felony obstruction, in which case they would be lucky to get a decade in a federal penitentiary."

"No," Francie protested, sensing he was exaggerating.

The FBI man raised his eyebrows and then laughed. "They'd be a lot luckier to have it dropped down to a misdemeanor and get away with probation and a fine."

"That would make more sense." She thought and then added, "But their talking to the right people could actually help your case, couldn't it?"

He nodded his head slowly. "That was my thinking. These are a bunch of good ole boys who have known each other for years and years. They have considerable feelings of loyalty."

"Maybe complicated by their intention to avoid as much punishment for themselves and their family. They're not going to go to the mattresses."

"Nope."

"And they're going to be thinking about who might be thrown to the wolves. And what might their role be in the throwing if it will purchase a better situation for themselves."

"They are only human. Like Suharto, who benefitted by both getting the mess off his own chest and serving up the actual perp...in a manslaughter."

Mike sighed deeply. "As the world turns and the dice are thrown." He scowled then smiled. "I thought there might be a useful turn of the phrase there." Francie winced. "But I guess not."

*   *   *   *   *

They had moved across the street to a coffee shop for a quick lunch after Ben Suharto had finished writing his account of what happened that fatal night, and subsequently related conversations, but hadn't been there long when Mike's phone buzzed. He touched an icon and brought the phone to his ear. "Olsen here." He listened. "Good. Put her in the conference room. Take away her phone. Search her for any electronic devices." Listens. "Yes, I don't want her pulling a gun out of her clothes." "Right. We'll be there in twenty minutes." He touched out, and to Francie said, "They brought in Megan Riels." He saw that Francie was about to ask a question and he answered it saying, "I know we're done and it's just across the street." He finished with a smile.

"But you thought you might let her stew for a while, out of communication with the rest of the world."

"Can't hurt. Want some dessert?"

"No, but another cup of decaf would be good."

Mike raised his hand, and when he got the waitress' attention, he pointed to Francie's cup.

*   *   *   *   *

On the way back to his offices, Francie offered to Mike, "You know, I don't have to be in on this, my friend. I just got involved to help Joella Jackson. We've done that. You don't need me, and I don't want to get in the way, or share your glory."

"Hah, I know you. You just want to go home, curl up on the couch with some bonbons and watch Oprah on the

TV."

They laughed together. "Listen, sweetheart, I want you in on this because first of all, you're the one who brought this case to me and brought it to a head. I don't care about plaudits any more than you do. I get too much praise and they'll try to move me to Washington for the umpteenth time."

"Well, we sure can't have that."

"Also, you are really good playing the good cop-bad cop by yourself. You get people so confused they're ready to pop in minutes."

Francie chuckled. "We do work well together, don't we, Mike?"

He opened the door to the lobby for her. "Yes, we do."

The FBI facility in Salinas was small, with six agents under Mike Olsen, one always in the office during weekday offices hours and one always on call if a case required more attention. The agent sitting behind the desk was the one who called Mike about Megan.

"Did you find anything on her?"

"A second phone; one of the throw-away kind. No weapons. She was not happy to wait without a phone. I gave her a copy of *Cosmopolitan* to keep her busy." He blushed slightly, and said, "I'm sorry, Ms. LeVillard. I didn't mean to sound sexist."

Francie laughed and replied, "You didn't. Anyway, if it's the one that was on the table here it was at least a year old, maybe two."

"That would make it current this side of the coastal ridge," Mike said over his shoulder as he waited for her at the conference room door.

It seemed likely that Megan Riels had been hired for her looks. She dressed to get attention, in what Francie later described as a semi-Valley Girl style. She was at the apex of San Benito County power as the chief aide to the county administrator. She made an effective Cerberus for Herbert Colossino, allowing access only to those who could benefit her boss and herself. That left him without a complete – or accurate – picture of some of the goings-on in the county, which is probably why he thought everything was running smoothly in his jurisdiction. That assessment was soon to be shattered...for both of them.

"Now Ms. Riels, I trust you signed the wavier and that you know everything that we discuss with you is confidential. And that you agree not to leave the county without written permission from the Bureau."

"Yes, but what is this all about, and who are you two?"

"I'm Mike Olsen, regional manager for the Federal Bureau of Investigation. The FBI," he added.

"I know what the FBI is. Who is she?"

Francie was letting Mike handle the girl, for she was very young looking, for the moment. "She is Francie LeVillard, the finest consulting detective since Sherlock Holmes."

Consternation and confusion swam around her face. Then she peered at Francie. "Didn't you tell Mol— Ms. Swinglet that you were gathering information to write an article about people in the water management field?"

"Ms. Riels, we'll ask the questions," Francie replied coldly.

"I want to call my lawyer," she said with a sneer and stood up. "I want my phone."

"Sit down, Ms. Riels," Francie told her in a no-nonsense tone. "I realize you must have shown some intelligence to get the job you had," she paused for just a moment for the verb tense to resonate, "but how smart are you that you are now facing hard prison time?"

Mike told her, "If you insist on calling a lawyer before we have a chance to talk with you, and hear your side of the story, then you'll be making that call from our main office in San Jose, where you will have been driven by one of my agents, under arrest, and in handcuffs."

The young woman tried to hold herself up to the veritable assault on her saucy denial, but her knees began to give and she dropped back in her chair.

"That's better," Mike told her and looked to Francie.

"Why did Ms. Swinglet call you about my conversation with her?"

"I, uh, well she was calling me about something else. It was about something about an agenda item at our next meeting."

"And how did her mention of my call come up?"

"She just told me about it."

"Was it typical that Ms. Swinglet would call you about all of her outside contacts?"

"Well, no, but –" Then she had another thought and rushed to get it out. "But she wasn't calling me, anyway. She asked for Herb – Mr. Colossino. He's the administrator. He runs things."

"But you were his chief aide. I would think in order to do your job, you'd have to know everything that came his way."

The aide had to consider her answer. "I told him everything but he didn't tell me everything."

"And what didn't he tell you about?"

She jumped on this one. "Well, how would I know if he didn't tell me?"

"No good, Ms. Riels. The conversation you had with Deputy Freylinghausn the other afternoon indicated that you were fully up to speed on what was happening to Joella Jackson. Did Mr. Colossino keep you in the loop on that one or did you know about it from other sources?"

Riels did not have a ready answer. There wasn't an acceptable one.

"If you were kept in the loop on that matter, it's hard to imagine what you didn't know about the administrator's portfolio." Francie used that word deliberately because she couldn't imagine it was one in the aide's lexicon, and would put her more off balance.

Megan Riels grabbed for a straw. Scrunching her face up, and in a wavering voice, she protested, "Look, yes, I knew about it, but I had to do what I was told. I wasn't responsible for all of this. He told me what to do. I was his employee."

Francie just looked at her. As she anticipated, a second shoe was to drop.

"Look, I have proof."

"Proof of what?" Francie asked.

"Memos and emails. And notes. I took notes. It wasn't my idea, any of it. I was just a confidential secretary, like. But I can show you."

Mike stepped in. "Where are those memos and emails and your notes, Ms. Riels? We'd like to see them."

"Well, mostly at my apartment."

Mike looked over at Francie. She looked back at the young woman but waited a long moment, watching her body English that suggested she thought the interview was over, now that she would be turning over her *proof*. Then in a more gentle voice she asked, "Megan, how long did you have an affair with your boss?"

The woman almost came apart at the seams. Her face blanched. "How did...? I never... Who told...?" She broke into loud sobs.

*   *   *   *   *

It wasn't difficult to get to see San Benito County Administrator Herbert Colossino. After all, it was Mike Olsen, the FBI regional manager, who was asking for the meeting. Plus the county rumor mill had already gone full spin about an investigation into alleged corruption between county leaders and business interests. The big question on everyone's mind was which scandal was about to break. Mike had phoned to find out when Colossino would be available, and the county executive had already had in his mind to clear his calendar as necessary.

The next question was where should they meet and that initially presented a problem. Colossino thought it might be at his office except that a few reporters and one TV news camera crew from San Jose had parked themselves at the front door of the county building. However, and not unreasonably, Colossino was leery of entering the FBI offices because that would certainly be noticed, and he didn't want to start this process knowing he'd have to bat down the flames of the gossip that would inevitably catch fire.

So Colossino recommended that they meet at the executive office of the Ridgemark Country Club where he was a director, and Mike agreed. Francie said she would attend, even though it meant she would miss her *aikido* training later that afternoon. A first *dan* black belt in the martial art, Francie trained three times a week, and as Mike knew, it was spiritual as well as physical exercise for her.

Colossino was waiting for them in the conference room. He was very cordial in greeting them, and when a waiter departed after they turned down an invitation for a beverage, his demeanor changed dramatically. In a strong voice on the edge of anger, he demanded to know why he was suddenly being regarded by friends and colleagues as a suspect in a corruption investigation.

Mike didn't answer immediately. Instead he looked across the table at the man, sizing him up. "Mr. Colossino," he finally said in a patient voice, "we are conducting an investigation, and that's why we're here, but I can assure you that we have never once brought up your name in any of our queries with other people." He paused and then said, "However you might have been referenced, it hasn't come from our office."

Slowly Colossino seemed to accept that. He turned to face Francie. "Excuse me, I should have held my displeasure until we were introduced." He stood up and offered his hand. "I'm Herbert Colossino, as you no doubt already know."

Francie stood, took his hand, and said, "I'm Francie LeVillard."

He squinted at her. "You're the detective."

"Consulting detective," she corrected.

"What does that mean?" he asked, sitting down as she did.

"Simply that I am not a member of law enforcement, though I often work with them in the pursuit of right and justice. I am also engaged by private parties for that purpose."

He was interested. "Is there a difference between right and justice, Ms. LeVillard?"

"I believe so, Mr. Colossino. One can find justice through the application of an outdated or badly written law, and in such a case right may be denied. If you have seen the film or play *The Winslow Boy*, this question is raised by the heroic Sir Robert Morton who defies the dicta of tradition and ultimately achieves exoneration for the wrongly accused Winslow boy."

"Most interesting, Ms. LeVillard, and how gratifying that you are present today as a participant in this matter. Thank you."

She nodded and turned to Mike.

"Mr. Colossino," he began, "I was drawn into this investigation when there were indications that county officials were working in collusion with the Southside Road Development Company to facilitate their building a new housing community. This came about because of alleged illegal treatment of people who were opposed to the development."

"If you are investigating Southside you must know that I am an investor in that project."

Mike nodded.

"But I made that investment a number of years before I assumed the position of County Administrator, and I have very deliberately kept my hands off of any decision-making regarding the project."

"Then who in your department deals with those matters?"

"I instructed my chief aide to hand them off as appropriate, whether they have to do with environmental issues it would go to one person, land use another, water a third. And I deliberately excuse myself from meetings whenever discussion on these points comes up."

Francie asked, "Was Megan Riels an appointment of yours?"

Colossino was surprised at the question but quickly covered it. "No. She had held the position under my predecessor who had only the highest praise for the work she had done for him. I saw no reason not to keep her as she had the institutional knowledge that would help me being new in the role."

Mike's phone gave a special buzz. He looked at it, excused himself, and left the room to take the call. When he was gone, Colossino said to Francie, "I must apologize for my earlier rudeness. With my last name, I feel I'm too often a target, of doubt perhaps, that people think I might be a member of the Mafia and organized crime."

"People do have their own filters, don't they?"

"Filters, what a polite way of describing discrimination." He sat back in his seat and smiled at her. "My father was very aware of such filters when he came to this country, but he didn't want to change our name. It represented an important family history that he wanted carried forward. But that is why he named me Herbert instead of Frederico, which was his name. He thought people would be less likely to wonder about my ethical character."

"I like that, Mr. Colossino," she replied, returning the smile. "It is not only personal for you, but it underscores the individual freedoms of our country."

"I hadn't thought of it that way, but of course you are right."

The door opened and Mike returned to his seat. "Sorry about that, but in fact it was very important to our meeting." He said to Francie, "I don't think you'll be surprised," and then turned to Colossino. "But one of our people at San Jose Airport stopped Megan Riels from boarding a plan to Mexico."

Colossino was clearly surprised.

"Was she going there on business for you?"

"Why no. We have no business outside the country."

"Might she have had vacation time?"

"No. I would have had to approve it and I hadn't." He thought a moment and it was obvious that he was putting the pieces together. "I'm inferring that Megan, Ms. Riels, has been involved in some matters that have drawn the attention of the Federal Bureau of Investigation."

"It certainly looks that way, Mr. Colossino," Mike told him.

"Oh dear. Then it would appear that I might have given her too much authority." He heard no argument. "Would you please tell me what you have found out? Not only should I know, but perhaps I can fill in some gaps for you."

Mike nodded his head and looked to Francie who then turned to face the man on the other side of the table.

"Mr. Colossino, we have to ask this. I think we already know the answer, but did you ever have a personal – to be more specific – an intimate relationship with Megan Riels?"

There was a brief but loud silence as he realized what

she had told them. Then he answered in a controlled voice. "Absolutely not. Not with her, not with anyone with whom I had a professional relationship. No behavior toward anyone that could be deemed in the slightest inappropriate."

"As I said, sir, we already knew the answer, but thank you for confirming it."

*   *   *   *   *

It was a year to the day after Francie busted Deputy Freylinghausn, so to say, on Airline Highway, and in a private dining room at the Ridgemark Country Club, the actors in this complicated drama were seated around a large table giving note to the past. Herbert Colossino was the host of the event and was standing at the head of the round table. To his left was Joella Jackson, noticeably wearing a fashionable pantsuit and her own nicely coiffed dark hair. To his right was Francie LeVillard dressed up for the event in slacks, a blouse, and a blazer; and no wig. I was to Francie's right with Judith Anne to my right, and Mike Olsen, who rarely attended such social events was seated on the other side of Joella.

"I'm most pleased that we could all get together to celebrate closure on the events that put our community under a cloud...a cloud that has been lifted by the hard work and smart thinking of you who sit around this table tonight.

"First, to Joella, who stood up to the powers that be in the name of what was right." After raising a glass to her, he looked across the table and said, "To Hollister homegrown Judith Anne who connected Joella to Tony who grabbed the ball and ran with it." Next he raised his glass to the woman next to him on his right. "To Francie who got the ball and took it to the goal line."

"What is this with all the sports metaphors?" Joella asked to laughter.

"This last one, please, Joella. And to Mike, who took the ball in for the score." With that everyone toasted everyone to muted cheers and broad smiles. Then Herbert regained his seat and an evening of chatter and mutual appreciation continued, lubricated by some of the finest San Benito County wines - don't laugh; they were quite decent – and a special five-course dinner designed with solicited input from the five guests. Yes, a good time was had by all. And when the evening was called, Herbert would drive Joella home since they were both locals, and the rest of us were limo'd back to Monterey County.

Which leaves it for me, Francie's chronicler, to provide the wrap-up of the game...er, the case. First, Megan Riels was in serious trouble, which was why she tried to flee the country. She was the brains, as much as there were any, behind the county's efforts to assist the developers of the Southside Road project. She did so solely for the exercise of power, in the vacuum created by Colossino's recusal from any business associated with the developers because he was a major investor. She thought she might benefit in some way for what she did for them, but it was the power plays that drove her. Drove her to prison. She being young, and her sobbing repentance before a judge who bought her self-reproach, she was given a year and a day in state prison, and five years' probation for corruption. More on her case in a moment.

Molly Swinglet pleaded guilty, out of severe guilt, to involuntary manslaughter. Letters from half the congregation of her Pentecostal church, all proclaiming her spiritual innocence, and her professed ignorance that Tom Finn ever even existed, along with the fact that she didn't ask for mercy, knocked down her prison time from three years to twenty months.

Ben Suharto was charged with obstruction and filing a false police report, but because he broke the case, the charges were reduced from potential felonies to misdemeanors and he was allowed to leave his job – which was really a loss for the county – and give up his pension, which was not inconsiderable.

And Deputy Freylinghausn also lost his job and his pension for misapplication of authority, but he got no prison time because the judge was remarkably lenient, based on the fact that the deputy wasn't profiting in any way except in the kudos he received from Megan Riels, on whom he had an obvious if unstated crush.

It also turned out his bulb wasn't as dim as it had seemed. An audio cassette – remember those? – arrived at the Salinas FBI office and it had a recording of a phone conversation between Freylinghausn and Megan Riels that pre-dated law enforcement interest in the two, so it wasn't captured by the tap. In fact, the contents of the call clearly illuminated Riels fostering the harassment of Joella Jackson, with chit-chat about how to make her back off of her opposition to the Southside development.

What a coincidence that the cassette landed in Mike's hands three days before he was to testify at Riels' preliminary court hearing. Because it was just a preliminary, regular rules of evidence didn't apply, so Mike didn't have to say anything about what came in the mail. Unfortunately for Riels, her lawyer opened a line of questioning that did her ill. He asked Mike how he knew that his client had colluded with the deputy.

"I heard them speak about it."

The lawyer was surprised. "But the recording made from the tap showed nothing of the kind. She was trying to shoo him away."

Mike: "I heard something entirely different."

Lawyer, startled: "What did you hear?"

Mike: "A conversation that took place several months ago."

Lawyer (smiling): "So you're telling us that this recording that you're referring to was not made under the authorization of the wiretap."

Mike: "That is correct."

Lawyer: "Then it was made illegally."

Mike: "I can't say."

Lawyer: "How did you obtain this recording?"

Mike: "From an unknown source through the mail."

Lawyer: "Then that raises the issue of validity. How could you be sure it was my client speaking?"

Mike: "I recognized her voice, and his."

Lawyer: "And you consider that authentication?"

Mike: "No."

Lawyer: "Then how can you be sure?"

Mike: "I had an electronics expert compare the recording to those that were made through our wiretap."

Lawyer (triumphant): "But if it was an illegal recording, and couldn't be used in court, why did you have an expert examine it?"

Mike: "Because we wanted to know if we were dealing with a fake recording which would then be investigated as another federal crime, an attempt to obstruct justice."

Lawyer: "But it wasn't fake."

Mike: "No, those were their real voices."

Lawyer: "So why did you bring it up?"

Mike: "I was answering your question."

As this point, Megan Riels stood up behind the defendant's table, and in a loud voice, declared. "I can't stand this anymore."

The judge told her to be quiet and sit down, to address the court only through her attorney.

"But your honor, he is no longer my attorney. He's an idiot. He's making me look worse than I am for having him as my attorney. I will represent myself from here on."

Her lawyer managed to say "But...but...but."

"Sit down, butthead," she snarled. Then she cleared her throat. "Your honor, this is all just a waste of time. My time, the witnesses' time, your time. I want to change my plea. I'm guilty. I did these things I'm charged with. I was foolish. I relished the authority I had and the power I wielded. I should be punished for what I did, but I won't evoke any further rancor for wasting anyone's time or effort trying to prove what I did. I did it. I'm sorry. I thank you for your patience."

And with that she sat down, sighed, folded her arms across her chest and stared at the ceiling.

Well, of course the tape came from the deputy. He had protected himself and effectively, and everyone knew it. Grateful for his illegal recording in putting the top dog in their lap, the prosecutors refused to file the misdemeanor recording charge against him. As a result, Freylinghausn was ordered to pay $25,000 to Joella Jackson for pain and suffering. He was able to keep his house, however, and after some time out of work, was hired as a security guard by the Southside Road Development Company.

The company didn't get off scot-free. There was no indication that they had paid for any of the favors they received from Megan Riels or the lethal intervention by Molly Swinglet. While the county had insurance to cover some of the cost of repairing the road when the water was released through the emergency discharge pipe, there was an extra cost for the larger water pipes that were opportunistically installed that benefitted the company, in the amount of $150,000. The company, wrapping itself in the mantle of nobility, agreed to pick up the tab.

Of course they would increase their profits by seven figures as the result of having more water to build and sell more houses, but there was no legal transgression in their actions. Molly Swinglet took the blame for her actions. She was never pressed to reveal where she got the idea to open the emergency discharge valve, or how to go about it. But that wasn't going to be prosecutable anyway. Someone might have speculated aloud to her over a drink what might be done, and well, it happened.

And this final note...Judith Anne learned from her Hollister-residing sister that Joella Jackson had been, as we used to stay, stepping out with Herbert Colossino. It's funny how life works.

Bang-Zoom

It was billed as an exploratory fundraiser for DeAnn Elsinour, the wealthy hedge fund manager emeritus who had decided to invest her success into politics. For a while she helped raise money for candidates, and then she founded the California Bipartisan Women's Coalition. Sort of like a California-only version of Emily's List but giving to candidates in both parties.

After several years of getting her name known around The Golden State, DeAnn decided to run for the U.S. Senate seat currently held by Dianne Feinstein. The 85-year-old Feinstein had had some health problems, and there were ever louder rumors that she would step down before her current term expired, probably in a matter of months, or simply not run again in 18 months.

DeAnn was ambitious and saw no need to politely wait for a formal announcement. She had never held public office, and wanted to get out in front of the half-dozen hungry Democratic members of the state's House delegation who would want a shot at the Upper Chamber, along with an equal number of the seriously rich Californians whose egos clouded their perception of their likely standing with the voters. Hence the event at her palatial home abutting the vineyard she had bought for her husband.

The action was not in the house but outside since the May weather on the east side of the coastal ridge in Monterey County was at its best. The manicured side lawn only slightly smaller than a football field was edged with tables of food and drink and festooned with American flags and pink-on-blue banners proclaiming the candidate's enigmatic slogan *DeAnn for Change*. At one end of the site was a riser with a podium, and standing behind it, the would-be candidate was wrapping up her welcoming remarks. A well-coiffed blonde in her early forties, of average height and carrying maybe a few extra pounds but well-dressed, she wore an earnest expression that implied she believed what she was saying.

"So I thank you all for coming. You've given me a real shot in the arm. You've persuaded me that this exploratory phase has revealed what it needed to. That you, and many Californians, want to be represented by new thinking in Washington. Not wild-eyed experimental new ideas, but getting back to basics. Cleaning up the environment, rebuilding America's middle class, and restoring faith in our government."

She paused for the expected applause, and then clapped her hands twice as if dismissing a class of fifth graders. "So please, enjoy yourselves. There's delicious food and plenty to drink. Have a good time. Thank you." With that she looked out at the 70 or so people who had been in attendance, and after a few moments, stepped out from behind the podium, came over to the edge of the riser, and shook the hands of the half-dozen people who had come forward to congratulate her.

Francie LeVillard had arrived just as the speech was about to start and had remained at the back and off to the side of the lawn. Her experience, cultivated by ten years of broadcast journalism, had taught her that she could see more from outside the crowd. During her reporting years, she'd also learned that remaining outside of the noisy reporter scrums that typified so many speeches and press conferences, she was more likely to be recognized by the speaker to ask a question as the forward crush was losing its energy.

In this case, however, Francie was not attending as a member of the Fourth Estate. She hadn't been active in journalism for more than a decade. Her last gig had been at the top-rated television station in San Francisco where it quickly became clear that the ratings were only about eyeballs, and journalism wasn't even an afterthought. When the station had to pay her off after their punk news director seriously misbehaved, Francie had ensconced herself in an oceanfront home at Yankee Point, a few miles south of Carmel-by-the-Sea.

It was through serendipitous circumstances that she had slipped into a new career, using the same curiosity, investigative skills, and demand for the truth that had been her requisite strengths as a journalist. In just a few years, she became known to the top people in law enforcement as the world's finest consulting detective since Sherlock Holmes.

But she had not come to the political event as a consulting detective. Several of her friends had suggested that she check out DeAnn Elsinour; they wanted to hear from Francie her thoughts on whether or not they should support her candidacy. Francie was also interested in seeing and hearing the woman up-close-and-personal because those same friends had suggested, based on her having covered more than a dozen elections, that she attend one of the Coalition's luncheons, to tell them if she thought the group was on the right track.

So the proverbial stage was set. Francie had listened to the speech and now she was wandering through the crowd – actually it was too sparse a number of people in such a large area to be crowded – to hear what people were saying about what they had heard. When she had first arrived, she stopped at a wine table for a glass of red that was the product of the vines that covered many acres surrounding the house. It turned out to be an unremarkable Pinot that she might have left on an unattended table, but she knew the advantage of keeping something in her hand to avoid shaking those of people she didn't know.

As most of the attendees had gravitated to the edges for food and drink, Francie prowled around behind them to pick up what she might overhear. Suddenly she found her way blocked, somewhat assertively, by a young man with a clipboard, pens, and contribution envelopes, and wearing a sash that read "Senator Elsinour".

"Hello, I'm Chip," he said somewhat urgently. He was on a mission. "Have you contributed yet?"

Francie shook her head, and said, "No, thank you." She started to walk around him but he moved in front of her.

"Oh, but you have to. She's so good. We need her in Washington."

"Uh-huh. No, thank you." Her energy was moving her in another direction, but this time Chip put his hand on her arm at the end of which was the hand holding the glass of wine.

"But this is a fundraiser. You came to a fundraiser. You are supposed to make a contribution."

Francie reached over with her free hand and removed his hand. Looking into his face with determination she told him, "That's not the way you treat guests, young man, especially those you want to support your cause."

Then she walked away. She thought she heard him say "Bitch!" under his breath but she didn't turn around to confirm it. With a minor effort, as she walked further, she put the incident behind her figuratively as well. When she had made a full circuit of the lawn, she calculated that she'd caught snatches of more than a dozen conversations and all but two were about the food – all favorable – and wine – mixed, at best. The other two were about the candidate.

"I don't know. She sounds like all the rest to me," said one thoughtful-looking woman with a disenchanted note in her voice.

The other comment was, "Not bad, you know. Maybe she can slip in if the others are, you know, too far right and too far left."

Francie was mulling over what she'd seen and heard over the past hour and was slowly heading in the direction of the parking area when an expensively-dressed man, a little over six feet, who probably spent considerable time at the gym, started walking beside her.

"You're Francis Villars, aren't you? I think I saw your name on the guest list." He stopped, and as if startled said, "But you don't have your name tag on." He smiled as though he thought himself important. "May I get one for you? Or perhaps you'd like to taste our special reserve cab." He smiled unctuously again and added in a lower voice, "It's better than what we're serving the hoi polloi."

"I don't think so, thank you," she replied, instead of saying what had come to mind.

"Oh, but Miss Villars, you must. You can't leave me with all these, these...I don't know. They seem like peasants, don't they? None of them can hold a candle to you."

"I beg your pardon."

"You are the best-looking woman at this whole show." He chuckled, "Although please don't tell my wife I said that."

"I wouldn't think of it." Francie said. "I don't know who you are or who she is."

"No," he said, overdoing his surprise. "She's the reason you're her. She's DeAnn Elsinour, the candidate." He smiled again and with pride said, "And I'm Leo Piscanti. This is my vineyard. I am Piscanti Wines. The talk is that Piscanti Wines are some of the best wines in California." He put his hand on her shoulder and gave it a soft squeeze. "You simply mustn't leave without tasting my cab."

"Take your hand off of me," she told him icily.

Disappointed, he did so, but slowly, and then she let him have it, perhaps flavored by some of her displeasure at the pushy fundraiser.

"If I were less polite, you'd be wearing the rest of this wine." She held it out to him so abruptly it might have spilled on him but it didn't. She shook her head. "What are you doing hitting on me, a guest at your wife's fundraising event? Are you trying to bury her candidacy before she even gets started?"

Piscanti looked confused.

"Let me put it another way," she continued. "How would you like it if a man treated your wife or sister or daughter the way you treated me? You would be outraged, wouldn't you? You have no right to behave like that. You should be ashamed of yourself."

Francie poured the remainder of the wine in her glass at his feet and said with a sharper edge in her voice. "And let me tell you about your wines. The Pinot you are pouring isn't even decent. It lacks character. There's nothing noticeable about it. And I can't say that I'm surprised, considered that you are Piscanti Wines."

She raised her eyebrows as if inviting a contradiction, and seeing none, she handed him her glass. Taking a deep breath and letting it go, Francie walked away from the man. As she did so, she noticed that two women who had been watching her talking with him, speaking in a very quiet conspiratorial huddle, and their eyes followed her as she headed for the exit. Her journalist's mind captured images of the two. One of the women was tall and taut, with gray-blonde hair and an athletic mien. The other was short and stocky and wore her dark hair in a long, thick ponytail. What most caught Francie's attention was that they were both dressed in loose jungle camouflage pants and black shirts.

*   *   *   *   *

The fundraiser was held on a Saturday. DeAnn Elsinour didn't wait until the beginning of the work week to call Francie. Her (home) office line rang at nine the next morning. Francie saw who was calling and silently gave her points for waiting until then but let it go into voice-mail. The message was business-like terse: "Please call me" and gave a number to call back. The number had a prefix that Francie recognized as secure. She didn't call back right away. Instead she went into the kitchen and made a cup of tea. While she was waiting for it to steep, she walked across the living area and through the French doors out onto the deck from which stretched an expanse of hard-packed sand and rock and unplanted gorse to the edge of the bluff that marked the edge of the Pacific Ocean. The view might have seemed plain to some, but to Francie it was every time revivifying, regardless of the time of day or clouds or distance to the horizon. This morning the marine layer hadn't yet made half the voyage to her perch, though with the convective air currents, she knew it was never far timewise from landfall.

She took a deep breath of the still air, feeling the ocean-borne freshness fill her lungs. There wasn't a day that she would be complete without such contact with Nature. She smiled at the thought and then turned and walked back into the house. She removed the bag from the cup and carried her tea into her office. She had written down the number, knowing that the call-back function wouldn't function against the security program.

She took a sip of the tea, and punched in the number. It was answered on the second ring. As her own system blocked Francie's phone number on the receiving end, the response she heard was a clipped "Yes?" It was barely a question. But it wasn't the voice she had heard from the podium; it wasn't even a woman's voice. Before she responded, the voice said, "Is this Miss LeVillard?" She didn't answer. He continued. "This is Leo Piscanti. Miss LeVillard, I am terribly sorry for the way I behaved yesterday. It was unconscionable. I am not the person who acted like that. I had, if you can imagine, over-dosed on antihistamines. My doctor had prescribed an extra strong steroid-based drug to get me through the afternoon outside and he told me only to take one. But it was such an important event for DeAnn that I didn't want to mess it up sneezing and coughing through her speech and meeting people, and so I took a second one." There was a deep breath. "And, to my deep regret and great embarrassment, you saw the result."

Francie's silence continued as she considered not only what he said but how he spoke. She admitted to herself that what he said was plausible. "Thank you, Mr. Piscanti. I'm glad you told me."

"Oh yes. I'm not that kind of person. DeAnn would never have married such a cad."

Francie chuckled. "Okay, Mr. Piscanti, you're off the hook."

"Thank you, thank you, thank you."

"Now did your wife set up the call for you or did she want to talk to me?"

"Actually both. She's right here."

In only the time it took to hand over the phone the candidate was on the line. "Let me add my thanks to you as well, Ms. LeVillard. May I call you Francie? I'm DeAnn."

"Sure."

"Besides my husband's drug problem–" she attempted a laugh "– may I ask what you thought of the event, and what I had to say? I know your background as a journalist, and I imagine you've covered a lot of campaigns."

"Candidly, I think you've got an uphill race. First because you're not from San Francisco or Los Angeles where there will certainly be candidates who start with an edge in media coverage. Second, while you're good on the issues, I didn't hear you set yourself apart from what we can expect from the moderate left. Third, I presume most of the people there yesterday already knew you or knew of you well enough to attend. But I didn't feel any excitement about you in the crowd."

Francie was going to leave it there, but instead told her of the experience with the fundraiser, adding, "I know this is a very early stage in your campaign, but not training the people who are asking for money is a critical problem. You don't call someone a bitch because she doesn't make a contribution. What is the expression about a frown goes around faster and more times than a smile?"

"Oh, lord," she moaned. "What else?"

"Well, you must know that running for office statewide is a moose. Especially in a state that's 1100 miles long with maybe 20 million voters with probably a dozen major different affiliations. You'll need ten million of them to cast their ballot for you. And you will need to spend, in a full-fledged campaign – win or lose – something in the neighborhood of $10 per voter or in excess of $160 million."

"I don't get your math."

"You're going to have to spend that $10 per voter on millions of people who are not going to vote for you."

"Oh right, yes, I knew that's what I was dealing with, give or take here and there. But is it winnable? Can I win the senate seat?"

Francie didn't respond immediately, and when she did answer, it wasn't what the candidate wanted to hear, except that she knew the woman wanted the truth. "Can you win? Yes. But there are too many factors to bank on being successful at this point. You don't know who else will run, what scandals will be reported, how low the candidates and their surrogates and the PACS will stoop. I can guarantee one thing, and that is, if you stay in until the end, you'll be a different person than you are today."

It was DeAnn Elsinour's turn to meet what she heard with silence, and when she spoke again, she was headed in a different direction. "I wonder, Francie, if you would be willing to talk to my group. The California Bipartisan Women's Coalition. We're having our annual statewide meeting here in Monterey the end of the month. Probably a few hundred people."

"I'm sorry, I don't do endorsements."

"No, no, I knew that. I was hoping you'd talk about what it takes to campaign in California. What you were just saying. I don't think most people, even in our group, have any idea the scope of the effort, not to mention the dollars, the miles, and the unmentionables. Or anything else. Whatever's on your mind."

Francie looked back on the conversation and smiled at the turns it had taken. "Possibly," she said, both of them knowing she said "yes". Which was confirmed when she added, "Send me the details. Time and place."

"And fee."

"You have my email address."

"Will do. And thank you, Francie," she said with feeling, "for everything."

*   *   *   *   *

As happens when life intervenes with plans, "yes" turned into "no" in a phone call to me, Francie's friend and chronicler. She was at a conference in Kennebunkport – Maine, six travel hours east, if you didn't know – and wasn't going to be able to get back to Monterey in time to deliver the luncheon talk the next day. Could I fill in for her? My answer was, of course, "Sure". It wouldn't be the first time something like this had come up last minute, and I was asked to fill in. Having written up some 50 of her cases, I had the speechifying goods where she was concerned. But I would need some information including when, where, to whom, and what was I supposed to talk about.

"Yes, of course, dear boy," she replied in a playfully hoity-toity tone since what I needed to know and what she was about to tell me was a given. "It's the California Bipartisan Women's Coalition, about a hundred members and maybe some guests. You're expected to speak for 30 minutes. You can talk about just anything you want. I was going to speak about the MeToo movement and how the situation has gotten waaay out of hand. You and I have talked about it."

"Yes we have, and while I think you would be able to get away with such a talk with mere muttering, I would be lynched."

"Nah," she replied after the briefest hesitation that acknowledged it was maybe a close question.

"Okay," I came back, with enough doubt in my voice to let her know I'd heard her meaning. "I'm certainly not thinking of taunting the audience. Although I'm glad it's a daylight event."

"You're very brave."

"I hope I don't have to be."

"Not to worry. I wouldn't ask you to step in if I didn't think you'd be a hit."

"Better to be a hit than be hit," I put in.

She laughed and gave me the logistics.

A semi-retired journalist myself, who stayed on top of the news, I had been noodling about the excesses of the various victimhood movements, as I referred to them. People were claiming offenses, real and imaginary, regarding gender, age, race, religion, and politics. The Black Lives Matters movement claimed that every black person shot by the police was an innocent victim. College students said they should be protected from ideas they didn't like; even to hear them mentioned. And there was the MeToo movement which got an important start over Harvey Weinstein and Bill Cosby but went overboard with Al Franken and the harmless tactility of Joe Biden. Plus people were filing complaints about relatively minor incidents that were decades old.

Worst were the hyper-liberals who saw sexism, racism, genderism, ageism, and new isms everywhere. And if anyone who wasn't of the victims' ilk talked or wrote about it – even fiction writers – they were damned for cultural appropriation. Publishers even had sensitivity editors to screen books; particularly for the Young Adult audience, to make sure there was nothing in forthcoming publications that might offend their target market. And to make matters worse, social media were fueling firestorms that burned reason at the stake. Filling in for Francie, I was going to get into all of that because while this was certainly her platform, it was one we shared. But maybe I would toss in a soupçon of Rodney King... you know, "Can we all get along?"

I've done plenty of public speaking to all sorts of audiences and always made it through to the end of my remarks. And these were politically-minded women, mostly professionals, who had come to the luncheon thinking that they were going to hear from the world-renown consulting detective, Francie LeVillard. Yes, they would be disappointed that she wasn't going to be their speaker, but I intended to keep their attention and leave them with something to think about. I thought briefly about writing the piece but decided I wanted the greater flexibility that speaking from notes would give me. I would be able to take the temperature of the audience as I went along, and stay on top of their interest curve. Ah yes, and again, the best laid plans, et cetera....

I arrived at the La Playa hotel ballroom at 11:45 to introduce myself to DeAnn Elsinour. Francie had, of course, called her to let her know of my substitution. I could see immediately that the woman was not happy that Francie had bowed out, though she'd had 24 hours to digest the news after Francie had called her. She had had no time to alert the members of the switch in entertainment, though she probably wouldn't have wanted to anyway, since it would have reduced the attendance. In any event she didn't have much choice. I was slightly irked that she wasn't more appreciative that I was available and willing to fill in, but I put a smile on my face with the thought that I might have told her, "Oops, I forgot that a *Monk* marathon is on the Hallmark Channel. See ya later, alligator."

The event was scheduled to start at noon with lunch being served. Association business would follow briefly, and I would talk at 12:45. After the announcement of my substitution was made at the beginning of their business, there was a not insignificant rustling in the audience, and I could feel cold stares cast in my direction. I was sitting at a table just below the podium, and in addition to Ms. Elsinour, there were eight other women, who talked primarily among themselves. I think I saw only three other men in the room, which was not a surprise and on some level was understandable. I kept a wan smile painted on my face, and quietly rued that the crowd was only bipartisan in political terms and not in gender. No wonder I didn't finish all of the meal but did down a full glass of Piscanti Chardonnay. When it was coming on my turn at the podium, Ms. Elsinour reprised the news that I was filling in for their scheduled speaker, and she thanked me for coming.

And my first words were to thank her for the opportunity to speak to such an august group. I apologized on behalf of Francie but her nation had called. Actually that was true. She was dealing with some significant issues at the request of, well, that doesn't matter. Suffice it to say that she would have returned and kept her commitment to the Coalition if her presence on the other side of the country hadn't been required.

I spoke about the polarization of Americans, and in important civil rights terms, gave examples of discrimination, as well as exploitation and abuse of new policies. If there were two sides in the audience, I was pleasing neither of them. When I came to the end of my time, and what I had to say, I closed with this.

"All of the issues of discrimination that have brought us to where we are today are about basic human rights. But if we continue to focus on each individual complaint, we neglect the over-riding need of the nation for unity. Surely we will be far more able to right individual wrongs when we are talking to each other in a civil manor with the purpose of assuring the rights of all

Americans. Until we are united again as a nation, we will fall short of that essential human goal."

Then I said, "Thank you," and looked down at my note cards. The applause started and slowly began to grow. I looked around the room at the faces at the tables. There were a lot of thoughtful expressions and a few enthusiastic. There were also a few angry enough not show basic courtesy even to clap unenthusiastically.

Elsinour got out of her chair applauding and came over to me at the podium, and said, "Well done, sir. Thank you." And then turning slightly to speak away from the microphone she asked, "Maybe you would like to work for my campaign?" I smiled and told her, "My campaign working days are long over."

There was a lot of handshaking as I made my way to the exit at the far end of the room. I was congratulated by some and appreciated by others. By the time I was at the door ten minutes later, most of the people had either left – many of them going back to work – or fallen into small groups to continue conversations. I walked out into the broad hallway and saw a woman coming in my direction that I almost didn't recognize. I had known Ursula DeVine for several years, but not seen her since she'd been promoted from Supervising Sergeant with the Monterey County Sheriff's office to lieutenant. I'd never seen her in civies before, only in her uniform.

She had been waiting for me to recognize her but when I did, her eyes opened wide, and she yelled, "Duck!" Which I did instinctively and watched a raw egg smash against the large windows on the other side of the hallway. Also instinctively, seeing that the missile had been thrown from behind me on my left, I jumped to the right and spun around, just in time to be missed by a second egg that smashed on another window.

That's when I saw the two women, standing on the other side of the exit door through which I had come out of the dining hall. I had noticed them at the back of the room because they were sitting alone, not at a table but together in single chairs against the wall. Also, they were rather under dressed for the event, wearing desert camouflage pants and beige tee shirts. I thought that perhaps they were veterans. They had exchanged remarks throughout my talk, while expressing displeasure with what I was saying in the looks they were shooting at me.

Now out in the hall and only 15 feet away, I saw the smaller of the two – she was darker, heavier, and less kempt – hand to her blonde and trim friend another egg. The taller woman drew back her arm to throw it at me when Lt. DeVine's voice froze her. "Sheriff's officer. Don't you dare." Underscoring her command was the fact that she had dropped into a crouch and was pointing her pistol at the women.

I sidled further away from her line of fire. I didn't know if the two might be armed. The tall woman put both her arms up, opened her fingers and let the egg fall to the floor. Her friend put her hands up, too, a deep sneer on her face.

"They're just eggs, copper."

"Yeah, it's free speech," snarled the tall one.

In a no-nonsense tone, Lt. DeVine ordered them to turn

around with their arms up and put their palms flat against the wall. The two women slowly complied.

"You all right, Tony?" she asked.

"Yes, thank you, Ursu — Lt. DeVine. Especially with you here."

"DeVine?" spouted the darker woman. "What a joke."

The blonde picked up the rant. "We didn't do anything. Just a couple of eggs."

"Yeah, and we didn't even hit him, so what's your problem?"

The two started lowering their hands as they turned around to face her. Lt. DeVine pulled back the hammer on her pistol. It made a loud click. "Turn around or I'll start adding felony charges to your arrest."

"Arrests?" demanded the shorter one as both women turned back around and raised their hands and put them against the wall.

Satisfied that they wouldn't move, Lt. DeVine relaxed her position, and with her pistol firmly set in her right hand, she took her phone from a pocket and pushed one button twice. It wasn't five seconds that she was talking to the sheriff's dispatch desk. "DeVine at La Playa. I need support. Two female arrests for assault."

"Assault?" the darker one cried out angrily. "You can't arrest us for assault."

Lt. DeVine listened to the dispatch desk then said, "Affirmative. We are in the main hallway outside the dining hall....Roger, thanks." She returned the phone to her pocket and informed me that Carmel PD would pick up the women very shortly. In fact, it couldn't have been thirty seconds that we heard a siren and it was close. And it was less than another minute that two of Carmel's finest were hustling down the hallway from the front of the hotel. They quickly handcuffed the two perps behind their backs, gave them a quick pat-down, and then a closer frisking. In another two minutes, they had been deposited in the back of their patrol cars and on their way to the local lock-up where they would later be picked up for transit to the county jail in Salinas.

"What was their problem?" she asked me. "Oh, and thanks for the name thing. I was made lieutenant ten days ago."

"Congratulations, Ursula. Well deserved."

"Thank you, Tony." She looked at the egged windows and the one that splattered on the floor when it dropped from the opened fingers. "It's funny with those two. They are deliberately nasty to law enforcement, and even to those of us women. "

"Maybe because you don't cut them any slack, for their gender," I wondered aloud.

She shook her head. "There's something wrong with them. Don't know what it is, but I am strictly by the book when I'm anywhere near people like that. I don't trust them."

"Crazy?"

"Maybe that, but also maybe evil."

She took out her phone and took photographs of the egg

splatters.

"Does anything happen for what they did, or tried to do?"

"You bet. They will be charged with assault and attempted battery to do harm."

"For throwing eggs?"

"It's a third degree assault, a misdemeanor, but you can get up to a year in jail for it."

"Oh my goodness. I didn't realize it was taken so seriously."

"Yes. They can do damage. Throw them against cars and they can cause dents. Also the whites of eggs can ruin paint on buildings and vehicles. People hit by thrown eggs have lost eyesight permanently."

Lt. DeVine had finished taking pictures and put the phone away. She pointed to the front door and we started walking.

"Thanks for warning me. And arresting those two."

"Always a pleasure seeing you, Tony," she said with a job-well-done smile.

*   *   *   *   *

"Oh my goodness, Tony," Francie said, her voice redolent with concern. "What did DeAnn Elsinour say about this?"

"I haven't spoken to her, Francie. I presume she's heard about it by now."

The silence on the other end of the phone spoke volumes. Then she confirmed, "But you weren't hurt, thank goodness."

"And thank Ursula DeVine. She was promoted to lieutenant. Which was why I didn't recognize her right away in civies."

"Thanks to her indeed. I would have felt awful if you had been hurt filling in for me." She was quiet and then spoke again. "I think the world is going mad."

"Yes. I think it's the too many rats in a box problem. Too many people, the stress levels rise, and a lot of folks can't handle it."

"There's another aspect to the over population, and that is that while the percentage of people going over the edge may remain the same, the numbers are growing, and dramatically, and that means more deranged people. And they affiliate, if not directly in person then through social media."

"And too many of them have guns, or will get them."

"Tony, do you think about carrying?"

"Actually, I do. I have my nice Beretta .25, my James Bond gun." I coughed slightly, and added in an authoritative tone, "Before he moved up to the Walther PPK so he'd have more stopping power."

"I suppose a .25 is all right if you are calm, you have time, and the target isn't moving."

"Yeah, I know. If I'm going to have a gun, I should know that it will do some good."

"Smart fellow. Need any help from me in this matter?"

"No thanks." I paused and then said, "Except maybe about one thing."

"What's that?"

"If I go legal, my name goes into an online file that lists all the people with concealed permits. That seems really dumb to me."

"Yes, dangerously so. Does that mean you wouldn't register for a permit?"

"I was thinking that way, yes. As our pal Phil Penko said, 'It's better to be judged by twelve than carried by six.'"

During her decade as a journalist covering her share of crime-'n-punishment stories, Francie had heard the expression more than once. She sighed and said softly, "It's hard to argue with that."

*   *   *   *   *

While Francie was not a religious person, she was very spiritual. She didn't believe in coincidence, nor god, luck, fate, chance, or accident. Her sense of what she referred to as "the larger reality" meant to her that if something or someone new or unusual showed up in her life, it very likely deserved her attention because it was very likely significant. So when Lawson Goodings texted her, asking if she might be coming to the Pacific Edge where he tended bar most evenings, her reply was, "Tonight?"

She climbed onto a stool at the otherwise empty bar at 4:45, as he was setting up his shift.

"What kept you?" he asked with a smile.

"How could I resist?"

"I thought you might like to try De Tierra's 2015 '5 by 5' Bordeaux Blend," he said pouring a generous amount into a glass and putting it on a napkin on the bar before her.

Francie made a show of looking over the glass before she picked it up. She held it to the light, swirled the contents around, and then enjoyed a long sniff of its bouquet before taking a good sip. The wine made its way around her mouth and then down her throat. The experience painted her face with appreciation.

"Umm," she offered. And in English, "Very nice. Alix did very good."

"I thought you'd like it."

"It was worth the trip itself."

Goodings laughed. "Yes, well..." His smile faded. "I don't know what you'll think of the reason I wanted to talk to you, but I felt with your sense of smell – smelling if something needs someone's serious attention – that I should tell you what I heard yesterday."

"Any time, Lawson. You're very discerning. What did you hear?"

He took a deep breath. They knew each other well enough that he didn't have to qualify to her for what he was about to tell her. "There were two guys at the end of the bar. In their fifties, local, successful. Doctors, I think, who play a lot of golf. They're in here every month or so. It used to be they came in with their wives for dinner. But they've been coming in without the wives for a while now.

"Anyway, they were talking for a few minutes and I wasn't really listening. Until I heard one of them say that he was afraid of his wife."

Francie pursed her lips into a silent whistle.

"Yeah, me too. It was like this afternoon. No one else at the bar, so I could hear everything even from the other end. He said his wife had been going to meetings for the past couple of months; a women's group apparently. At first, he said, his wife would tell him that they talked about politics, mostly women's issues that the husband wasn't terribly interested in, EMILY type stuff. Then the husband got a hard look on his face and told his friend that his wife had stopped talking about what was said at the meetings. In fact, she didn't talk to him nearly as much as she used to. She'd been a chatterbox, but now she was barely talking to him.

"The guy had hit a tough point. He finished the back half of his martini and signaled me for another one. He didn't say anything until I put it in front of him. He put his hands around the glass and looked at it. Then he turned to his friend and said that one night, maybe two weeks before, he woke up in the middle of the night, and opening his eyes he saw her looking at him with an angry expression on her face."

"Oof. No wonder he was scared."

"No kidding. But it got worse two days later when, he told his friend, he heard his wife on the phone – not knowing he could hear her – talking to a girlfriend about whether to buy a Glock 19 Gen 4 or a Ruger LC9s. She said she wanted something EDC.

"Francie, do you know what EDC means?"

Francie shook her head. "I think I heard the acronym but I don't remember what it stands for."

"I guess the husbands knew about guns, but it wasn't until they left that I looked it up. It means *Everyday Carry*. It means that the gun is small enough to be concealed but has *assailant stopping power*.

"We're talking two guys with money, nice homes, and ten-year marriages at least. And this poor guy is scared of his wife."

"And it sounds like he should be."

"How did the other guy respond to what he was hearing from his friend?"

Lawson thought a moment. "He was a little displaced, if you know what I mean. It was new to him. He didn't think it affected him, but he wasn't sure."

Francie swirled the wine in her glass slowly and then took another big sip. "Two final questions, my friend. Do you have names of these men, and maybe the wives, and can you describe them, at least the one who was scaring her husband?"

Lawson picked up the bottle and poured Francie a generous second glass of wine. Then he gave her the information she'd asked for.

*   *   *   *   *

The call from the sheriff's office wasn't a surprise, except somewhat that it was from the sheriff himself. Telford

"Bogie" Spivac and I knew each other fairly well, mostly because of my relationship with Francie and writing up her case histories, but also because during the times we had been together, we'd established a friendship of our own. It came easily because during my years as a broadcast journalist, I'd had plenty of contact with law enforcement, at all levels, and I could quickly tell those who were serious about justice and not just being one of the gun-badge-'n-uniform clique.

"Hi, Bogie, I bet I know why you're calling. Ursula did a great job yesterday."

"Thanks, Tony. She's one of the best I've seen in eighteen years."

"You want me at the arraignment tomorrow, I presume."

He chuckled. "You do know the routine, don't you." It wasn't a question. "Yes, it's going to be in Monterey so you don't have to come all the way over here."

"Thank you."

"And I don't think you'll even be called. You can probably just sit in the back of the courtroom and make notes for your next novel."

"Novel? As busy as our friend is, I don't have much time to write up anything but her work."

"She does keep busy, that girl does. Okay, 9:45 in courtroom six. It shouldn't take more than twenty minutes. And again, I don't think you'll be called, but in case the wrong judge is sitting or they get some shyster who attacks DeVine, you could be back-up."

"Glad to do my part. Those two are whacko. I hope they're given LWOP."

The sheriff laughed. "For a third degree misdemeanor, seems appropriate. Anyway, thanks for being there. And I'm looking forward to the next time we can clink glasses of Sierra Nevadas."

"Sounds like a plan. Take good care, Bogie."

*   *   *   *   *

The next morning I got to the courthouse early. It was cloaked in the thick grey marine layer which might burn off in the late afternoon, or it might not. It was damp, so instead of walking around outside for a bit, I went inside. Through security and then to courtroom six. I sat down in the back and looked around. The judge had been on the bench handling administration issues for the past hour, but there was still a dozen or so people waiting for the preliminaries in their cases to be heard. A few minutes before my matter was to be called, I saw Lt. DeVine enter on the other side of the courtroom with one of the assistant DAs. She saw me and her eyes said good morning. After a short conversation with the ADA she came over and sat down next to me.

"You really do pick 'em," she whispered to me.

I looked at her half askance.

"They got Dick Pyright to represent them." She looked at me to confirm that I knew the man.

"High-priced smarmy."

She nodded. "The perps want to make a federal case of this though they don't have anything to work with. They refused to bail themselves out, even though it was only a couple of hundred dollars each."

"Oy."

"No kidding."

"What's their defense?"

"Free speech."

I started to laugh but caught myself.

"They picked the wrong judge. Candy Postman is a rock-ribbed conservative. She reveres the Constitution. She's going to find this insulting."

"And Pyright is letting them do this?"

"I don't think he can control them, and anyway, aside from the exorbitant fees that he charges, all he's interested in is ink."

"One of those. He doesn't care what the press says about him as long as they spell his name right."

"That's him." She looked up as the ADA caught her eye. "Gotta go. Enjoy the show." She got up to join her at the front of the courtroom.

"Thanks, Ursula, for today and especially for the other day."

"Sure."

Shortly afterward, the door to the detention area opened and out came the two women who had assaulted me, so to say, wearing prison orange and accompanied by a bailiff. They looked altogether too cocky as they dropped into chairs at the defendants' table. After talking to their attorney, they turned and looked around the courtroom. When they spotted me, they got animated and the tall blonde raised her arms as if she was aiming a rifle at me. Then she put down her arms and smiled at me. I found her expression profoundly unsettling.

I was glad that I wasn't the only one to witness this. The ADA and Lt. DeVine showed surprise and concern at what they saw.

But that was the only excitement. The hearing was very cut and dry. The ADA asked Lt. DeVine what had happened. Dick Pyright said that the women had exercised their First Amendment rights to free speech. He said that his clients wanted a jury trial, and he asked that they be released in their own recognizance.

The judge frowned at the lawyer and shook her head. She told him he was whistling by the graveyard and wasting the taxpayers' money. Then she set bail at $1,000 each, saying that considering their addresses they could afford it, and maybe it would teach them to show more respect. Then she told him she would get back to him with some possible dates.

Judge Postman was about to close the case when the ADA stood up and asked that, in light of the assault and lack of contrition, the judge order the women to stay at least 500 feet from the victim. "So ordered," said the judge and banged her gavel.

*   *   *   *   *

"You needn't apologize, Francie," DeAnn Elsinour told her. "What you were doing back east was more impor-

- 180 -

tant than talking to our group. Although I know they would like to hear from you." She stopped then but remembered what else she wanted to say. "Tony Seton was very good. What he said got people's attention and got them to think. Even a number who were disappointed that you weren't there."

It was almost a week after the speech-cum-egg-throwing and she had persuaded Francie to meet her for midmorning coffee at États-Unis. Francie had begun by repeating her regrets at her last-minute call to bow out of the speaking engagement, and while she was slightly put off by the woman's implication that she knew why Francie had done so, she didn't let it show. She presumed that Elsinour knew one of the upper-level financial people who had been at the conference, and she didn't like playing games so she skipped ahead to her own purpose to agreeing to meet.

"I'm glad you got to hear Tony. He's very much on top of the news, and his take on the social upheaval we're experiencing is most enlightening." That earned her a sincere nod. "By the way, were you aware of what happened after his talk?"

The blank look response said she didn't. Francie cocked her head in surprise. "Hmm. Two of the attendees of your event were waiting for him and when he left, they threw eggs at him."

"No!"

"Yes," Francie said, though she hadn't needed to. "As it happened, one of the sheriff's top people was walking by and saw the whole thing. She had them arrested.

They were arraigned on assault charges."

"Oh gracious. He wasn't hurt, was he?"

"No, the lieutenant shouted for him to duck, he did, and they missed him. Thank goodness."

Francie was taken by how shocked the woman was. She must lead a very ordered life, she thought, seeing her expression move toward contemplation.

"And they were from our event?"

"Yes, Tony had seen them sitting against the back wall. They weren't at a table."

"I wonder if they were supposed to be there."

Francie said, "I couldn't say, but I think they were the couple I saw at your exploratory fundraiser last month. They were off to themselves then, too. They were wearing jungle military fatigue pants and black shirts. Tony said that at his talk they were wearing desert camou."

A light went on in Elsinour's eyes. "Yes, I know who you're talking about." She nodded and sighed but didn't add anything.

Francie looked at her pointedly but when an answer was still not forthcoming, she was not surprised and she asked for the names. Relenting, Elsinour told her. They were the names of the two women who were arraigned for assault. They were also the same names Lawson Goodings had given her.

"Have you had any issues with these women before, De-Ann?"

The woman didn't answer, not immediately, but her silence did. Francie thought to push her for details but instead thought it would be better to hand this over to higher authorities. Though she had an unexpected lot on her mind, Elsinour didn't have anything more to say at the moment, which was fine with Francie, and they soon departed. From her car, Francie made a call to set up a meeting for later in the day.

*   *   *   *   *

"You didn't think Tony should be here?" Mike Olsen asked. He was sitting with Francie and Sheriff Spivac at a corner table at Tarpy's far from every other customer. Not difficult since it was three in the afternoon.

Francie answered, "I wanted to know what we're dealing with before I worry him."

"That sounds reasonable. What do you have?"

"I made a couple of phone calls, and Ariane checked some of her sources. It looks rather ugly. Darlene Morley and Myrna Carsteen were members of a group called the Pebble Beach Militia. You both have known about them. It's a group of a dozen or so of hardcore women from Pebble Beach who enjoy guns, and do target shooting at their own private soundproof range one of their members built in her basement. There are some additional members who like to get together socially every month to talk about guns, have shooting contests, drink sports tea, and eat pastries. It's good we know at least that much about them, but regrettably, some of their membership files were corrupted so we don't have complete information on them.

"Morley and Carsteen are members but they haven't been to the meetings in a couple of months. They haven't formally withdrawn but they were known to complain that the PBM wasn't edgy enough. They thought the group should be doing some outreach to increase their numbers to have some real clout. And I don't know if this matters, but Carsteen may have once worked as a personal aide to some mercenary CEO. Not Erik Prince at Blackwater USA, but someone like him. She was also in a brief relationship with a former Special Forces sniper. Anyway, most of the remaining members were glad to see them go. Some thought the two were more than edgy; maybe crazy, misandrists; they hate men. The two have developed a very close relationship, and at the same time, their marriages seem to have been headed for the rocks. They spend a great deal of time together.

"Neither of them has a criminal record, but they have been to dark websites that talk about revolution, torture, automatic weapons, and survival gear, food, and hiding from law enforcement." She stopped there. "That's mostly it." She took a sip from her glass of Chardonnay.

"And they wanted to attack Tony because?"

"They never made that clear. They just said that they had the right of free speech. And their form of speech was guerrilla street theater ."

"What's your take, France?" The sheriff asked.

"You guys know me. I don't get all antsy, but there's a smell to this whole situation. I think I told you I saw those women last month, and there really is something wrong with them. It's like I can tell there's a story here, and it's bad news."

"What do you want to do about it?" Mike asked.

"Well first, to let you know what I know..."

"Including your roused olfactory sense."

"Yeah. Also, I think these two may think of themselves as a two-person team of trouble. I don't think they're getting input from anyone but each other. Some sort of spiritual joining. Maybe a kind of love, and they want to show themselves off in a political way. Or at least as being women trashing men." Francie grimaced. "I feel responsible for Tony being in their sights because he filled in for me – took the place of a woman – and that's not all right with them. He made a good target."

The sheriff spoke up. "When their attack failed, rather spectacularly, it probably just upped the ante for them to want to go after him again."

Francie nodded. "That's what I'm worried about."

*   *   *   *   *

If the bullet had come any closer, I wouldn't be here to tell you I heard it. A 30-06 165 grain Nosler Custom Trophy Grade bullet, which it was later determined to be, travels at 2800 feet per second. Sound travels at 1,125 fps. That means if you are within a half-mile of the muzzle, as I was, and hear the shot fired, the bullet had gone past you a half-second earlier. Or in other words, the bullet would have hit you before you heard the shot fired.

There was no point in dropping to the ground. Unless a second shot was on its way. Not likely at that distance, but why stand there and wait to find out if this case was an exception. I hit the ground behind a bush and quickly wiggled forward several feet to be behind thicker under-brush. Just in case the shooter thought to fire low to where I had dropped, thinking I might be just wounded.

I may sound somewhat pedantic in writing about it now, but I knew exactly what was happening when I heard the whiz of the bullet go by my right ear. I had just turned my head because I thought I caught a glint off something out of the right edge of my vision. That's my point about how close it was. It missed my head only because I turned it. The sound of the shot catching up had removed all doubt about what I had heard.

Without producing much movement, in case the sun might glint off my phone, I punched in a unique three-digit code that had been given me only a few days earlier. About the time the bullet was landing in the ocean four miles out, Francie was answering, "Tony... Go."

"Someone just shot at me. Rifle with a scope, probably from a house near the southeast corner of Carmel Meadows. I'm on the path, about two-thirds of the way up the path from the Whisler-Riley houses to the top of the hill, lying behind some brush. No second shot."

"Got you," she said after a moment, and I could hear clicks and beeps in the background. I was to learn later that my phone signal had been triangulated to within three yards, and Francie had forwarded my location to the sheriff's tech trackers.

She stayed on the phone with me, making sure I was un-harmed and not going anywhere. It wasn't three minutes after the shot had been fired that I heard sirens coming from both directions on Highway One. They kept getting louder until one from the south stopped at the bottom of the hill by the houses behind the Bay School, and at almost the same time the siren from the north turned off onto Ribera Road continuing in my direction.

"Company's coming, Francie." I knew she could hear the sirens through my phone. "One down by the Whisler's, one up here, coming to the top of the stairs."

"Don't move, Tony. When you hear them coming near you, call out softly so they aren't surprised and fall over you."

"Right."

"Keep this line open with me until you're safe."

"Right."

I knew she was afraid for me and to reassure her I said in an even voice, "France, I'm alive and unhurt. Really." Her silence said she knew I was all right, at least for the moment, but the situation would need serious attention to be resolved, and for me to be safe from any further attempts on my life.

"Francie," I said with some urgency, "He missed me because I turned my head at the last moment."

"And?"

"And you know how we are only looking at three-thousandths of what our vision captures. Well I think I saw a glint, maybe off the rifle, the scope, or something near it, a window."

"Where?"

"The end of Cuesta Way. Maybe the second house from the end. Highest second floor view."

"On it. Stay down."

I could hear Francie relaying what I said, and at the same time I heard someone calling out my name. Not loudly but evenly. For the briefest moment paranoia struck me and I wondered if it was the person who shot at me. Logic intervened as I told myself the person couldn't have gotten so close to me, and not have been seen in the open ground between me and where the sheriff's deputy car had screeched to a halt maybe 75 yards away.

I spoke up. "I'm okay. I'm lying on the ground on the path. Maybe 30 feet from you." That was something of a guess, based on the sound of the voice, but it turned out to be close. Moving cautiously, two deputies reached me in less than ten seconds. One of them hunched down next to me to cover me while the other called the other deputies who were climbing up the trail from the other side.

"I'm good, Francie. The troops have arrived."

*   *   *   *   *

"I think it would be a good idea if you were out of sight for little while. Until we can collar these two."

The advice came from Francie as we sat in her living room. The deputies had walked me back to my car, checked it over to make sure nothing had been attached to it, and then driven behind me in a cruiser to Francie's house, per her instructions. She lived just past the Highlands, a few minutes away from where I'd parked.

"Stay here or get out of town," she added.

"How long are you thinking?"

She made a face. "They aren't pros. I think they'll catch up with them quickly."

Her phone rang. She read the display. "It's Bogie," she said. "Hello, Sheriff, Tony's here. Shall I put you on speaker?" In response, she pressed a button and put the phone on the table.

"Hi, Sheriff," I said. "Thanks for the rescue. Your people were great."

"Glad we could serve, Tony. Now we'll find whoever is after you."

"Did you find where they shot from?"

"Yes. It was where you thought. The second house in from the end with the second floor. The house was empty and being painted for the new owner. There were no alarms set so the painters could come and go. Someone broke the lock on a sliding door in the back of the house. Then went upstairs. There were some marks by an open window that I think will test positive for gun powder."

"Good work," Francie put in. "I presume you're canvassing the neighbors."

"Yes, although so many of the people up there are part-timers. Still, it's Sunday and some of them are here for the weekend." The sheriff spoke away from the phone. "No kidding," they heard him say. "Go get what you can." He chuckled. "So to speak." Then he was back with us.

"You're not going to believe this but we think whoever it was used the bathroom while she was here."

"'She'?" Francie asked.

"Well, not to sound sexist, of course, but the seat was down."

We laughed.

"Bogie," Francie said, excitement in her voice, "when the women were booked into the jail the other day, you swabbed them didn't you?"

"Yep, everyone is photographed, fingerprinted and swabbed. And yes, we'll see if there's a match. That would all but lock in a conviction. Okay, gotta go. More when I know."

We thanked him and Francie disconnected the call.

"So where are you headed?" she asked.

"How 'bout Mendocino?"

"You should be able to stay out of trouble there for a few days. Why don't I fly you up there? You can stay at my house; you've been there before. I have a car in my hangar there."

"Sounds like a plan. And I have two days of clothes and a phone charger in a bag in my car."

"You Boy Scout you."

*   *   *   *   *

I spent the first few hours after I landed walking through the woods above the ocean by her house, trying to clear my mind. From my early journalism days into my current professional life, principally as the chronicler of Francie's case histories, I was quite comfortable playing the observer, staying above the fray. This being a player – and a target – was not to my liking. I looked forward to hearing that Darlene Morley and Myrna Carsteen were behind bars. That night I slept better than I had in more than a week.

The next morning I made the effort to push all thoughts about Monterey away as soon as they surfaced. I spent hours sitting on the bluff high above the beach, watching the ever-changing skies and ocean, listening to waves and gulls. I had deliberately left my phone in the house. My mind needed cleansing. Finally hunger got the better of me and I headed back. There was a message from Francie, telling me there was no news and wishing me well. I responded with an email so she would know all was fine up here. Very fine.

As wonderful as were our situations down on the Central Coast, there was something about Mendocino that was specially different. There were fewer people most of the year, and while she had all the important amenities of life here, there was a rustic feel to the area. Also, the locals were there, not for work or just retired, but to live, and often to practice their art. The people here produced beautiful paintings, photographs, leather goods, and wood carvings. While they sold many of their works to visitors, now through the Internet their markets had expanded globally, giving them more reason to stay put.

Speaking of artists, there were a number of the culinary variety, first-rate restauranteurs who had relocated to the area. They did very well when the tourists were in town, but as the success of their friends grew through online sales, the local customer base grew to healthy levels. No one got tired of the year-round delicious farm produce, and what the fishermen brought to the docks that could be on plates only hours from the sea.

There was something else about Mendocino. Virtually everyone I encountered there – and Francie shared the feeling – were people who we would look forward to seeing again and again. They were thoughtful and gracious, and they engaged the people who came to see their art or enjoy what came out of their kitchen. Not everyone, of course, and with the disinclined, they didn't intrude. Just with those who reflected their values. After a second night of rich sleep, I woke up smiling and appreciating why Francie had a second home here.

*   *   *   *   *

Francie flew up to Mendocino to bring me home. She laughed when she saw my face at the airport, standing by the office, looking as relaxed, she told me, as she had ever seen me...and then some. "Mendocino will do that to you, won't it?"

I smiled. "Hard to hide, but who would want to? And," I said as I put my bag and then myself into her plane, "your house has an extra dollop of whatever it is that discharges the tension, anger, annoyance, disappointment – whatever – that plays such a serious role in the so-called real world."

"Such as life on the Monterey Peninsula is real."

"There's that." I strapped myself in and put on the headset to lessen the noise from the engine and to let me communicate with Francie during the flight. I also liked to listen to the talk with Air Traffic Control. Less than a minute later we were lifting off the runway, and soon we were on our southeast track to Monterey.

"I was thinking we might stop in Shelter Cove for lunch but I got a call from DeAnn Elsinour. She asked to meet with me at three. She thinks she can persuade Morley and Carsteen to turn themselves in."

That struck a discordant tone somewhere in my being, but I kept my voice even as I asked, "Where are you going to meet?"

"She wanted it to be at her place, the winery, but I wasn't interested in driving all that way, especially because the ride home would be rush-hour traffic on 101. So she agreed to meet me down at the Mission at three."

"I didn't know she was Catholic."

"Her husband is. Reform, but he's taken her to some of the special events like Easter and Christmas."

If we had been speaking directly to each other instead of through the headsets, Francie might have heard the doubt in my voice. And if I hadn't gotten so relaxed over the past three days, I might have pressed the issue. But up to that point, I was feeling unrestrainedly peaceful and I didn't know if I was over-filtering what my feelings were saying.

"Do you need company?" I asked, still evenly, but it still brought a look from her.

She didn't answer immediately; she was re-checking her thoughts. "No, thank you, my friend. I'm just talking with DeAnn. We're not taking them in."

I nodded. Not that I was fully satisfied, just that I'd deferred to her.

The flight down was delightfully quiet and beautiful. With a slight tailwind, we made it to Monterey in an hour-thirty, maybe fifteen minutes early. Francie had already pulled my car out of her hangar and parked it by the fence next to her own. I helped her push the plane into the hangar and close up, and then we went our separate ways.

After putting dirty clothes in the hamper and re-packing my two-days-worth of fresh togs for the bag in the car, I sat down at my computer to catch up on what I hadn't wanted to deal with when I was in Mendocino. But during the 45 minutes or so since I got home, I had found myself checking the time every few minutes. At ten of three, I gave up the ghost of my concerns and acted on them. I slipped the Beretta into the front pocket of my loose jeans and headed out. When I arrived at the Mission, I saw Francie's car parked toward the south end of the building, near the children's baseball fields. I made a U-turn and parked on the opposite side of Rio Road and then walked back across the street. I was headed to the courtyard when I heard her raised voice coming from the side of the courtyard where deliveries were made, and I moved quickly in that direction.

When I got to the corner of the building, I put my head

slightly forward so I could see what was happening. Then I saw Francie and Elsinour about thirty feet away, standing ten feet apart.

"You had no right," Francie said with anger and concern. She was also looking around in all directions, and carefully backing up toward the building. She could at least protect her back.

"Too late to worry about that," said Darlene Morley as she stepped out from behind a gardening shed on the other side of where Francie had been moving. Francie stopped because the woman was holding a large automatic with a silencer pointed at her.

"Darlene," said Elsinour sounding parental. "Put that down. You agreed to turn yourself in to Francie if I brought her to you."

"Come on, DeAnn. Don't be stupid. You're the only one who bought that. Even the star detective here knew the moment you told her I was here what was going to happen."

"No, Darlene. This is wrong," declared the erstwhile senate candidate, taking a step toward the woman.

Morley's gun spit once, and Elsinour, struck in the chest, spun around and fell to the ground, her head hitting the pavement hard. At that very moment, I either somehow saw or felt a heavy strike coming to the left side of my head. Some part of me knew I couldn't escape the blow, but I still had enough sense to go with the strike so that it jarred me but I didn't lose conscious as I fell to the ground.

But Myrna Carsteen didn't realize that. She grabbed the

collar of my jeans jacket and pulled me just inside the delivery area and dropped me on the ground by the wall. I managed to land so that my hands were down by my legs and then I didn't budge.

"Hey, we got a twofer, Colonel," Carsteen called to her friend.

"Good work, Major," came the reply and they both laughed.

The tall blonde walked over to her friend. "So what are we going to do?"

"What we had planned. We could have had more fun at the vineyard, but we don't have the time here. Too busy."

Francie told me later that she knew I was still in the game and she needed to get their attention on herself. "What is your problem with me? I'm on your side. We have the same politics."

The short, dark "Colonel" was pointing her gun in Francie's direction, her hand moving around as though it was looking for a target. "What is my problem with you? You mean, beside the fact that you saw me shoot that bimbo?" She nodded to the silent heap that was DeAnn Elsinour. "Even if you were on our side, as you call it, you can't fix that." She nodded in my direction. "Or that shot that we took at your friend last week." It sounded like she was addressing me with that line.

But then I could hear from the tenor of her voice that she had turned back to face Francie. I carefully opened my eyes part way and saw where the three people stood.

"Major," the dark one ordered, "go get the car. Bring it all the way in here."

"Right, Colonel," the blonde said, and I could hear her jogging out of the delivery area.

That would give me some time, and if Francie could keep her talking for a minute, it would have to be enough. I slipped my hand into my pocket, which was not in Morley's view. I pulled out the magazine, edged a bullet from the clip and slipped it into the tilt-up barrel. Then I replaced the magazine with the other seven rounds because I didn't trust my aim that I could take her down with only one shot. I had practiced this routine in the dark more than once, and the situation I was in wasn't dissimilar. All my attention was focused on my fingers. I couldn't drop anything. I had to move quickly. I couldn't make any mistakes.

I knew Francie wasn't looking at me, as it would certainly have drawn Morley's attention to me, but it meant that she wasn't seeing what I was doing. But she was doing her part, trying to give me more time, keeping up the conversation.

"But why did you want to shoot Tony? His politics are more left than mine."

"This isn't about politics. Left, right, whatever. Your friend..." – I froze at the reference – "...got us arrested and put in jail."

"He did not," Francie said demonstrably. "It was the sheriff's lieutenant. She saw you throw the eggs. And why did you do that anyway? I heard he gave a good speech and got some decent applause."

"Yeah, and so what. You were supposed to be there and he took your place."

"But it wasn't his choice. I couldn't make it back from the conference in Maine in time to get back. I asked him as a favor."

"Yeah well we didn't know you weren't going to be there. Otherwise we wouldn't have come. We didn't want to hear some guy."

Francie kept at the conversation. "I have to ask, at the fundraiser, the way you two were watching me and DeAnn's husband, he acted very badly with me and it seemed out of character. Did you give him some kind of drug to make him act foolish?"

The woman guffawed. "You guessed that, did you? Yes, we spiked his drink, his own lousy Pinot. And you weren't the only one he hit on. There were some others, too."

"But why, why did you do it?"

"Because he was a man, and really full of himself."

"But he was her husband. I thought you were supporting her."

The woman was tired of talking. Hatred resurfaced in her face. "Enough," she growled.

"How did you know that Tony was going for a walk that day?"

Morley laughed her cocky pride. "We had plans for him and were keeping an eye on him. One day when he was at the post office, he left the window of his car partly open. His running – walking – shoes were on the back seat. We slipped a tiny chip under the footpad. Bang-zoom."

Francie sighed her distress. "Is there anything I can say that you would let us go? We haven't done anything to you. Lock us up," she nodded toward the gardening shed, "and get away. We won't do anything for an hour."

"I'm not dumb," Morley averred. "You wouldn't wait a half-minute 'til you were calling the cops. We don't need that hassle." There was the sound of a car revving up on the other side of the wall at the end of the delivery area. The woman chuckled. "Myrna does love that car." She looked back at Francie. "Time to go." She raised the gun toward Francie but then changed her mind. "Wait. I think we'll send your friend on his way first. So you can see him go."

Morley turned slightly and brought the gun around to shoot me. That's when she saw my Beretta pointed at her. I had already pulled back the hammer, and now holding the pistol as steady as I had ever held anything, I pulled the trigger twice. She was hit twice, in the stomach and chest, and doubled over.

At almost the same moment there was the screech of brakes as Myrna Carsteen pulled up at the entrance to the delivery area. She jumped out of the car, and screaming out to Morley, ran to her friend. I was on my feet in a crouch tracking her with my gun. I didn't see that she had a weapon.

Francie had drawn the Glock from the holster under her jacket on the back of her belt and was also following Carsteen. The woman was crying now as she helped

Morley, bent over, to the ground. Francie ran towards the two, gave Carsteen a hard push that knocked her away from Morley and onto her backside. Then she kicked Morley's gun, which had fallen in front of her, in the opposite direction. I ran behind her and picked it up by the barrel, flicked on the safety, and shoved it in my belt.

Francie kept her gun trained on Carsteen who was wailing at her friend, who was crumbled on the ground and not moving. "Tony, keep your gun on her," she ordered, pointing her gun at Carsteen. Then she pulled out her phone and punched three buttons. The emergency line was answered immediately.

"Bogie, The Mission delivery area...The two women... One shot serious...Also DeAnn Elsinour shot serious...Need ambulances and officers...Tony and I are all right." She paused. "Acknowledge." She said to me in a calmer voice, "Help is on the way." Then she went over to check on DeAnn Elsinour.

She bent down, looked at her face. Her eyes were open and vacant. She put her fingers on the woman's throat to feel for a pulse. It didn't take long to confirm that she was gone. She stood up and came over to Darlene Morley. First checking to make sure Carsteen wasn't going to move, Francie then checked the woman for a pulse. It didn't take long. She stood up and looking at me, shook her head.

I had kept my eye on Carsteen the whole time until Francie stood up, and in that moment, emitting a wild, angry growl, the woman shot to her feet and launched herself at Francie. She and I both fired at her at the same time. My bullet caught her in the shoulder but didn't slow her down. But the 9mm bullet from Francie's Glock hit her in the neck and severed her spinal cord. With her arms reaching for Francie, her body flopped down on the pavement two feet from Francie.

We just stood where we were for maybe ten seconds. Until the sound of sirens roused us from our subdued state of shock. Francie confirmed that Myrna Carsteen was dead. She took a deep breath and let it out. The sirens were less than a minute away. Francie put her gun back in its holster on the back of her belt, and then she pointed to Darlene Morley's automatic. She took out a handkerchief and retrieved it from me. I carefully let down the hammer on the Beretta, flicked on the safety, and put it back in my pocket.

Lights flashing, its siren dying, a Carmel PD car pulled up with a sheriff's car right behind it. Two police officers and a pair of deputies got out of their cars, one of each moving forward toward us carefully while the other kept cover behind their car door. Francie and I remained still. "I'm Francie LeVillard. I called in the shooting to Sheriff Spivac."

"Yes, ma'am," said the lead deputy. "He told us you were good. He's on his way. He was in Monterey and should be here in a couple of minutes." He turned back to his partner and told him to let the sheriff know that they were on scene and the situation was secure.

The Carmel officer came up by the deputy and stared at the corpses of the three women. She looked seriously unsettled. She signaled to her partner to come forward. When her partner saw his fellow officer's face, he gently took her arm and headed her back to their cruiser. She got back in the cruiser and could be seen on the radio.

She was back in a minute with some more color in her cheeks. Speaking to the sheriff's deputy, she said, "Uh, we were dispatched as closest to the scene, even though the Mission here is beyond our jurisdiction, but with the situation stable and with you here and the sheriff on his way here" – she looked around and saw the sheriff's car coming up Rio Road – "well, we'll be on our way."

The deputy nodded his agreement and the police officer returned to her car and they slowly drove off. Sheriff Spivac got out of his car just as two ambulances arrived. He came over to Francie and me, looking us up and down to make sure we were all right. He took the gun Francie had been holding and handed it to his deputy.

She explained, "That's the gun that Darlene Morley used to kill DeAnn Elsinour." She pointed first at the killer and then at her victim. "And this is Myrna Carsteen. I'll give you the details later, but so you know. Morley had sent Carsteen to get their car on the other side of the Mission and was about to shoot Tony and me. But Tony shot her first. Not a minute later, when she brought the car around and saw what happened to her friend, thinking I had shot her friend, she tried to get at me. We both shot her at the same time, but my shot killed her."

The sheriff and his deputy were silent. Finally the sheriff spoke. "We'll need your firearms to test."

"Of course," Francie said, and slowly drew out her pistol and handed it to the deputy. I followed.

"Larry," the sheriff said to his deputy. "Let's get these

guns processed and back to them this afternoon, if we can."

"Yessir," the deputy said and put them in a locked case in the trunk of his cruiser.

Alone with Francie and me, the sheriff let out a deep breath. "My god, what a horror story. Thank you, Tony, Francie. You not only saved your own lives, but who knows what these two might have done before they were caught."

The deputy returned and the sheriff told him, "Have the ambulance people hold off until we've got all the photography we need. Lieutenant DeVine was down Carmel Valley and should be here shortly. She will take control."

"Right, sir. I think that's her unmarked coming now."

"Good." To Francie and me he said, "When the lieutenant is here, I'll have you walk us through what happened, though it looks pretty clear, that nothing was moved. Then maybe we can get together for dinner? I'll see if Mike can join us."

Francie looked at me. "I think we would be up for a drink, don't you?"

"Drinks plural," I replied.

*   *   *   *   *

The four of us were sitting in the Captain's Room, a glassed-in private dining area at Edgar's at Quail Lodge. We agreed to put off talking about the day's events until after we'd enjoyed the first round of drinks and some appetizers. It was a good idea. It let us sit back for a while, talk about other matters that might draw some smiles. It worked, letting us approach the fatal five minutes that left three people dead, outside the Carmel Mission of all places, with a degree of emotional quietude.

Mike Olsen had gotten much of the story from the sheriff who had remained on the scene when Francie and I had recounted the events to him and Lt. DeVine who was managing the case. I looked at Francie and suggested, "Why don't you tell what happened, since you were the first there and the only one who had her eyes open the whole time."

She nodded. "Okay, I got a call from DeAnn Elsinour this morning, telling me that she thought she could get Morley and Carsteen to turn themselves in. She wanted me to come out to her place in the valley but I declined and she agreed to meeting me closer to home, by the Mission. She must have thought that she could get the two women to turn themselves in, and to me," she shook her head in disbelief. "I don't know how she could have been so wrong about their intentions."

"I knew immediately when Morley came out of the shadows holding a full-size automatic with a silencer what the game was. I had come armed but there was no way I could get my gun out without being shot first. When Elsinour got into an argument about their purpose, I had a moment to think. But then Morley immediately lost her patience with her, and almost without a thought just shot her. It was then that Carsteen came back from parking their car on the other side of the Mission, and she saw Tony peeking around the side of the building. She knocked him on the head and carried him into the delivery area, dropping him next to the wall." She stopped and looked at me.

I nodded. "I had sensed something was wrong when Francie told me about her plan to see Elsinour, and I finally gave into my concerns and went to make sure she was all right. I was upset enough to carry my Beretta .25 in my front pocket."

"Thank goodness," put in Francie, and she patted my shoulder.

"I don't know how I knew it, but I had a sense that a blow was coming to my head and I turned it quickly just as she struck me, deflecting some of the force away. Enough so that I didn't lose consciousness, but I pretended to be out, thinking that I would be ignored. Which I was for a while. And that gave me time to ease the gun out."

The sheriff had pushed the regulations and returned Francie's and my guns when he arrived at the restaurant. I took mine out and showed them how I had taken out the magazine and put a bullet in the tilt-up barrel.

"I didn't have a lot of time. Morley had sent Carsteen to get the car, and she was going to dispatch Francie and me before she got back. Francie kept her talking for a bit, just enough time actually, and just before Morley was going to shoot Francie, she decided to shoot me first. She'd been focusing on Francie, and when she was turning toward me, I rolled over slightly and fired two shots." I looked to Francie.

Francie nodded and picked up the narrative. "It may have been only a .25 but the bullets hit her in the stomach and the chest. I had taken out my gun, and it was timely because Carsteen arrived. She saw Morley bent over and ran to catch her, easing her to the ground. I got to her side and shoved her away and back onto her seat. Tony kept a gun on her and that's when I called you," she said to the sheriff.

I added, "She was shrieking like a banshee and bawling when Francie tried to find a pulse. When it was obvious Morley was dead, Carsteen flew at Francie but both of us – I don't think we expected it but we were ready – shot her and she fell to the pavement."

I paused, looked at Francie who shook her head, and said, "And that's all we wrote, so to say."

The waitress had seen from our four faces that we didn't want to be interrupted, but after we had finished our tale, it was clear that our collective mood had lightened up. Still, she knocked on the door and was summoned in to take our dinner orders. Francie also ordered a bottle of Prosecco, very cold, and Bogie told the waitress to put a second bottle on ice.

When she left, he said, "I'm not sure what to say, or think, about us being together tonight. Part of me wants to celebrate the fact that this screwy case is over, or the incredible heroics you two showed and the fact that you are both alive. On the other hand, it was tragic that three lives were taken."

His comments were greeted with thoughtful silence. Then Francie put her hand on my shoulder again and in a strong but gentle tone said to me, "My dear friend, you don't have to speak to this, but I was wondering how this affected you. Not to invade, but to make sure you are all right." She shook her head. "Not all right. Very well."

I looked at her for a long moment and then clarified. "I do feel well, Francie. And I think you mean, how does it feel to have killed someone?"

She nodded.

I paused, looked at Mike sitting across from me and then Bogie next to him. "It is something that may take a while to digest, but maybe not. I seem to process quickly unless I feel a need to argue with another part of my mind." I chuckled. "If that makes sense." There were knowing nods around the table. "Okay, first, when I was lying on the ground getting the bullet into the barrel and the magazine back in the grip, I wasn't thinking of anything but what my fingers were doing."

I turned toward Francie. "When I heard Morley say she was going to have you see me die before she was going to kill you, I was planning how I was going to line up the shot, that I would point with the second knuckle of my trigger finger of my right hand." I raised my hand, and pointing away from the table, showed them what I meant. Then I added, "I had no thought of killing her. It was just to protect Francie. And when she turned toward me, the only thing in my mind was to be rock steady through the second shot."

I took a deep breath and let it out easily. "After that, my only thought was on Francie being all right, and then dealing with Carsteen. I didn't let my mind embrace the fact that I had very deliberately killed a human being until I was home, taking a shower.

"There was some synchronicity involved here. Just last week I had a conversation with a friend I've known for four years who had been a Marine in Vietnam. He said no one he knew over there ever talked about what it meant to kill someone, but he said, and I wrote it down, 'Initially it's an absolute feeling of power.'" I let that sit for a moment and then went on.

"He also said that when there was a large-scale attack, when the Marines bolstered the Army, the Marines spread out with three Army between them. That was because the Army were reluctant to shoot, and the Marines knew that was why they were there. I recalled to him that S.L.A. Marshall had written that 82% of the American soldiers in the Second World War never fired their guns at the enemy."

I stopped there when I saw the waitress at the door with our Prosecco. We were silent as she came in. Francie told her she was sure it was fine and that she should pour. Which she did and left.

"I'd just like to say a few more words to finish my answer to you," I told them, "and then we can decide to what we are raising our glasses." There was acceptance around the table. "During my chronicling of Francie's amazing career, I never asked her how she felt about shooting someone, but I didn't have to. In recounting the events, she expressed her feelings. Especially the time she was in the hot tub...yes, we all know that. And the time she fired through the window against that Eastern European woman who was going to kill the young man from the storage units. And the Russian assassins. There was tremendous poignancy in those moments. And when she was ready to kill the guy at the school who killed that wonderful professor and he had a large knife to kill her. She was flooded with emotions."

I put my head back on the high back of my chair for a couple of seconds and then returned. "You know, I never thought to ask either of you guys what it was like for you to have killed someone. I guess I thought you somehow took it in stride; that it was part of law enforcement. And I'm not asking now. And maybe that's how I'll be. There was not a single case of Francie shooting someone who didn't really, really deserve it. I presume the same with you, Bogie, and you, Mike. That's certainly the way I feel about shooting Darlene Morley. I saved my own life, and Francie's. I don't think of myself as heroic. I didn't get a kick out of doing it – about losing my virginity, as it were."

I turned and looked at Francie. There were tears in her eyes, and now in mine. "I love this woman. I would do anything for her." I held my glass out toward the middle of the table and the others followed suit. "To Francie, the person who brought us all together, doing right." The glasses clinked, the Prosecco was sipped, and the four friends shared one of the brightest and most joyful evenings of their lives.

*   *   *   *   *

It was three days later when the phone rang and it was France calling. We had spoken numerous times since the fateful business at the Mission, of course, and gotten together a couple of times for conversations with law enforcement, and just to connect.

"Good morning," Francie said. "I trust I'm not calling

too early."

"No, you're good," I told her. "I've usually been at my desk for an hour by this time."

"I know. I'm on your news list. But sometimes people can be awake and not ready to engage in a conversation."

"Hah! Yes that's true, but you never disturb me."

"Except when I go off to meet someone who's setting me up and not telling the truth."

"Didn't a red flag go up for you, Francie?"

I could hear her deep sigh.

"You know, it did, but I thought it wasn't what it turned out to be. First of all, I thought she didn't understand what she was getting into. And second, I didn't think I was the one to arrange their turning themselves in. I mean, I thought she could have generated some good press for herself if she did it. And that's what I was going to tell her."

"Got it. Well, I'm glad I listened to the alarm I couldn't turn off."

"How's your head, Tony? That was very neat that you were able to shy away from the full brunt of the blow."

"It's a little tender...nothing serious. But thanks, yes, it was neat. I've been trying to think of what I heard or saw or sensed and I haven't gotten a picture of it yet."

"I wonder if it wasn't something like your seeing the glint that caused you to turn your head and the bullet whizzed past."

"I wouldn't be surprised if there was a connection."

She asked, "Any guess how they might have known you would be on your walk?"

"It may be in how you asked it. It was my walk. Maybe they heard me saying something about it. And when they saw me park by the Day School they got into position. Something we'll never know." He added, "Or have to."

"Of course," Francie acknowledged. "By the by, did you get the text from Bogie, about the sniper position?"

"No. I don't text much and rarely check. What did he say?"

"You're going to love this. Apparently Carsteen did relieve herself before she shot at you. The DNA at the house matched her intake swab at the jail."

I laughed sardonically.

"Not funny but ironic," she observed.

"Yeah, and I've got another one for you. I ordered the Smith & Wesson a week ago."

"The M&P 2.0 compact?"

"Yes. You said you'd fired a box with one at the range and liked it."

"I did. Nice piece. So the irony?"

"I didn't have it with me because the waiting period had a few days to go."

She jumped on it. "Oh my god. So you had the Beretta which fit in your pocket and you were able to get it out which you wouldn't have been able to do with the

S&W."

"That's right."

There was something of a silence, and then Francie, with a very different tone in her voice said, "Hey, what do you think of flying up to Mendo for a few days?" She stopped there and when there was no immediate answer, she continued. "You know my house. It's plenty big enough. We wouldn't have to stumble over each other."

"Maybe meet for meals?"

Francie's laugh was soft and warm. "Well, maybe."

"What time shall I pick you up?"

"I'll pick you up, my friend. You're on the way to the airport. And I'll stop and pick up some food on the way. Anything special you'd like?"

A thought crossed my mind, but I nixed it and said, "No bell peppers. Not hot about mushrooms. But almost anything else. Lots of salt and grease."

There was that lovely laugh again. "I'll get food for me and a couple TV dinners and Ramen noodles for you."

"Oh yum. I'll be ready when you get here. And France, this is a marvelous idea."

*   *   *   *   *

We took off into a fog layer but were above it at 3,500 feet. We had leveled off at 6,500 feet and as we made our way up the coast, the grey beneath us began to dissipate. By the time we got up to the Golden Gate, it had backed off several miles from the shore.

"Would you like to fly?" Francie asked.

"I'd be glad to take it if you want to relax."

"I'm good, but you used to fly."

"Yes. I may take it up again. I have to say, we have very similar styles of managing this plane. I watch you respond to radio calls, clouds, wind. It feels like I used to fly. You wear the plane and fly it as though it's a part of you."

She gave a me a big smile. "I do love to fly. It requires, and receives, pretty much of my full attention. I look around a little bit, talk to you, but control of the aircraft is intrinsic."

"Ah, that's a great way of describing it. Yes, sure I'll fly a bit."

"You have the plane."

"I have the plane."

When I gave back control of the aircraft to Francie for the approach to Little River Airport and landing, I was pretty sure that if anyone was tracking our flight over the half-hour I was flying, they wouldn't have seen any perceptible different in the way she was flown.

*   *   *   *   *

Landing at LLR, I unpacked our few bags from the plane along with what Francie had picked up at Bruno's for us to eat, and I put them in her car which she had pulled out of the hangar. Then, attaching the push bar to the front wheel, we guided the aircraft into the hangar. We locked it up, and I offered to drive. It produced a wide smile on her face. "You were reading my mind."

I went around to the passenger side, opened the door for her, and closed it when she was comfortably inside. I got into the car and we headed off on the ten-minute drive to her house. Though the ride was short, and familiar to both of us, we could feel our comfort levels rising in every moment.

I took us down the long drive that hid the house from the road and pulled up by the front door. "Why don't you open up the house, and I'll bring the bags in?"

"Okay, but just bring them into the house. The food is all wrapped in ice packs so they can wait. Let's go for a walk along the bluff."

"Wonderful idea. You have your walking togs on, so do I. We're ready."

It took three trips to carry the bags and boxes from the car to the house, and in the meantime, Francie opened up the blinds on glass doors that opened onto the backyard and a view of the ocean through the spaced out pines and cypress trees that topped the bluff. She opened one of the doors, and walked out onto the deck.

"Should I heat up the hot tub, France?"

"You roué, you." She laughed. "No need. I turned up the temperature through an app on my phone after I called you."

"How convenient, said the roué."

We stepped off the deck and onto the well-worn, but not tired, path that wound through a garden of natural plants that garnished the back yard. Then the path took a turn through the trees and along the top of the bluff.

The sun was still climbing but there was a soft breeze coming over the ocean that made us glad we were wearing light jackets. For the first hundred yards or so, no words were spoken. I knew there was something on Francie's mind but didn't push her to tell me.

Soon, without any further preamble she began, "I've been for the past few days, since the Mission, thinking some new and compelling thoughts."

I had no idea where she was going with this but her voice was sure and vibrant.

"I realized, my dear friend, that even though we've known each other and worked together, very success-fully, all these years I didn't really know you." She looked at me to make sure I was hearing her. "Of course I liked you and certainly respected you, both profession-ally and personally. Right off I knew you to be a good person."

"Excuse me. Look," I said, pointing to a flight a pelicans traveling only a few feet below us, following the coast-line.

She looked. "They are so graceful."

"Sorry, I didn't mean to interrupt. I didn't know if you had seen them."

"No I hadn't. Thank you." She gave me a long smile, then she took a long breath and let it out softly. "What I was realizing, dear Tony, is that I hadn't really known you as a man. And what I saw in you that afternoon – first that you decided to check up on me, and then the rest. No," she corrected herself, "I want to be specific. How you somehow partially dodged the blow from

Carsteen so you would keep conscious. Wow. I know you said you didn't know how you knew the blow was coming, but somehow you did and you stayed present. Then how you managed to fall on the ground so you could get your hand into your pocket, take out the Beretta, and make it ready to fire.

"And then, Tony, how, lying half on your back you fired those two perfect shots that stopped Morley from going ahead and killing us. Finally, being so sensitive to Carsteen, you knew of her attack and fired and hit her. Yes, my shot stopped her, but she wouldn't have been difficult to fight off with your bullet in her shoulder.

"Anyway, it was about more than the fireworks. It was also how after you calmed down so smoothly and dealt with the police." There she stopped as I did with her, and she turned to say this to me directly. "But the capper, Tony, was how you described what had happened at the dinner with Mike and Bogie. There was such merit in what you said. That you didn't shoot Morley to kill her, you fired to stop the assault on me. It wasn't to save you it was to save me. You said, 'I love this woman. I would do anything for her.' Suddenly I saw you in a new light, a different you. And not to sound trite, Tony, but I was blown away inside."

I knew Francie had finished what she wanted to say, since we were suddenly walking again. But I found I didn't have words to respond in that moment. Maybe because I had said them – she had quoted them back to me – and I knew I would certainly repeat them again and again. It didn't matter. Our hands brushed, and then they took hold of each other. We managed to take a few steps further and then we both slowed to a stop and turned to face each other. Our lonely hands found the other. Our eyes plumbed the depths to each other's soul. And then our lips met.

When they finally parted – it wouldn't be for long – I pulled my head back only far enough to have the lovely face of this extraordinary woman before me in focus I observed to her, "Francie, I think this is the beginning of a beautiful friendship."

"And I think we should head back to the house. I think I saw a bottle that needs to be opened."

With that we kissed again, and then joyfully, wordlessly, we rewound our path. Back in the kitchen, I pulled a bottle of Veuve Clicquot out of an ice pack and announced, "It's still cold. Perfect."

Francie opened the freezer and pulled out two frosty flutes. I carefully removed the cork, producing a nice pop, and then poured the champagne. I handed the first glass to Francie and picked up the other and raised it to her. Her eyes widened as she remembered something. "Didn't you tell me of the toast that Archie Goodwin made to Lily Rowan in one of the last Nero Wolfe stories. Oh, I can't remember it."

"May I?"

"Yes, please."

"He said, 'To everybody, starting with us.'"

"Yes, that's it." Her smile broadening, she raised her glass.

"But I wonder if we shouldn't have our own words.

Especially for this special moment."

Her eyes sparkled. "You have some in mind?"

"How about, 'To the new us'?"

Her eyes brightened. "Very good. To the new us." We clinked glasses and sipped the champagne.

I put the champagne in an ice bucket and brought it over to the living room area where we made ourselves comfortable on a large couch that sat behind a coffee table and looked out to the west. The sun was now overhead, bright on the backyard and the ocean to probably ten miles out where our view was blocked by a thick marine layer.

"So Francie..."

"Yes, Tony..."

"Do these new thoughts move you in any particular direction?"

"Uh, yes, Tony."

"Would you care to share them?"

She cleared her throat. "This will probably seem rather sudden, and maybe it is, but I thought you might be interested in sharing living expenses."

"Oh my, really?"

"Like mortgages, hangars and other flight costs."

"Taking turns picking up the tab for dinner when we go out."

"Uh-huh."

I reached for the bottle and filled our glasses. Then I

asked, "Do you see any arguments for not proceeding in this new direction?"

She shrugged and sighed. "You know, I can't. I mean, we can't use the excuse that we don't know each other."

"Not after ten years."

"Ten years and not a complaint," she confirmed.

"Real or grammatical," I said with faux pride.

Francie laughed.

It was a lovely sound. My heart took hold and my voice softened. "Oh my dear fr — ...Francie, I was about to call you my friend. I have some terrific and important relationships with men friends, as you know, but you've always been more than a friend. You mesh with me emotionally and spiritually. We finish each other's sentences. We're not competitive. I feel in you a deep well of trust, of affection, of purpose."

Francie took some time to absorb the feelings that carried the words. She tried to put on a serious face when she said, "I know we both prize our privacy. We'd have to make sure we protected that, I think."

"Oh, yes, that would be important," I volleyed.

"But having a house here and one at Yankee Point, I think we could manage. And we could get a second plane."

We laughed together and I offered, "Somehow I don't think that will be a pressing issue, at least for a while."

Francie raised her glass to me and said, "To a very long while."

There was another clink of our glasses and a swallow of the champagne. Then I took Francie's glass and mine and put them on the table. Then I lay back on the couch and pulled her on top of me.

About the Author

Tony Seton is a journalist, writer, publisher, public speaker, business/political consultant, and communications specialist. As an award-winning broadcast journalist for ABC TV, he covered Watergate, six elections, and five space shots. And he produced Barbara Walters' news interviews, and Dan Cordtz's business/ economics coverage.

Later, Tony wrote and produced two award-winning public television documentaries. He has conducted over 2,600 interviews and is the author of more than 2,300 essays.

Through Seton Publishing, Tony has written and published more than 45 of his own books and screenplays, and edited and published 30-some books for clients.

As a political consultant, his clients have included Nancy Pelosi, Tom Campbell, John Vasconcellos. the American Nurses Association, and an abundance of local candidates.

He has taught journalism and writing, provided media training, and produced websites.

Tony is also a private pilot and a photographer.

SETON
PUBLISHING